MISTLETOE AND THE BILLIONAIRE'S COWGIRL

COWBOY CHRISTMAS, THE MISTLETOE COLLECTION BOOK 3

EDITH MACKENZIE

For every cowgirl and cowboy out there. Don't let your past define your future

CHAPTER 1

CHRISTMAS, ST MORITZ

*W*ho *says money can't buy happiness?* Markus watched the attractive brunette strip down to her bikini to join him in the hot tub. *Merry Christmas to me.* A mere couple of yards from where his hands languidly draped outside of the swirling water, thick snow drifts began before a frozen lake spanned to the very edge of the white-capped alps majestically rearing up above. *It really did make a man feel like he was insignificant,* Markus thought, his mouth twisting into a smug smirk. *Unless you had enough money to buy those mountains.* Appreciatively, he watched as the woman—*what was her name again?*—seductively dipped a toe in the water, the steam thick between them as she slid the rest of her lithe body in. Cynically, he doubted the distance would last very long.

Somewhere in far off Colorado, Quinn was getting married to that hick cowboy of hers. It was her loss really.

Who would want to live a life in the muck of livestock when she could have slept on silk sheets every night—w*ell, maybe not always sleeping*—and her days being pampered? Markus rubbed the bridge of his nose, still irked by her rejection. It wasn't like she was ignorant of what he had to offer. He'd taken precious time to show her and still she'd acted like he was no one. Heck, last Christmas he'd even bought a casino to show the woman how much he wanted her.

Never again. He smiled, gesturing for the lovely brunette to come closer. *No names, no promises. That was the way to live life.*

~

THE SLEEK TOWN car pulled away from the curb outside the restaurant, a blonde and a brunette seated on either side of Markus, his arms draped lazily around the giggly pair. Outside a Christmas market set up in the square flashed into view.

"Oh my gosh, can we go there?" The brunette giggled. *What was her name? Maybe I should get the other one to say it.* Markus dismissed the thought as completely ludicrous. Like he cared what her name was.

"I'll have the driver stop the car." He motioned for the man to halt, and she giggled even more with childlike excitement as they came to a standstill and the driver stepped out to open her door. She quickly slid out, stopping confused when she realized that no one else had followed. *I guess it wasn't her brains that got her into the car in the first place.*

"Aren't you coming?"

"No. But do enjoy." Markus smirked as the driver shut the door on her. Horrified at being so unceremoniously dismissed, she began to tap on the window. She appeared to be saying something, but all he could make out was her mouth flapping.

"Do you wish me to continue to the chalet, sir?" the driver asked, careful not to make eye contact. *It was good when the hired help were well-trained in how to act around their superiors.*

Markus squeezed the blonde who had remained beside him, now sitting frozen as though unsure what was going to happen next. "Do you have any suggestions you'd like to make?"

Her eyes skittered to his. "No. Whatever you want is what I want to do."

He patted her on the head. "Good girl. The chalet it is."

Markus didn't give the shivering brunette another thought as they sped off, leaving her cold and standing in the gray slush of the gutter. He had more fun things to focus on.

"MERRY CHRISTMAS," Lachlan, the manager of Markus's casino, The Chimera, said. Markus could barely hear him over the raucous noise in his suite. There were girls dressed in naughty Mrs Claus outfits and elves, men dressed as reindeer, and one fellow asleep in the corner who appeared to be a candy cane. Empty bottles of Cristal were strewn about the room.

"Why are you calling?" Markus wanted to return to the decadent overindulgence that was his Christmas celebration, and the dull little man kept for his outstanding ability to kiss up to him was bringing him down. The blonde on his lap needed his full drunken attention.

"I wanted to inform you that Kelly has extended her Christmas break by a week. I was sure you would want to know." He could almost imagine the sly gleam on Lachlan's face as he tattled on the absent PR manager.

"I assume you told her that wasn't acceptable."

"I did, and she told me to go suck on a candy cane!" Pure indignation bristled down the line at the affront. Kelly's choice of insults did amuse Markus, but he still didn't like the opinionated woman. *Heck, I don't like my women to have an opinion full stop.*

"Perhaps it's time to start thinking about our options with her. A man wouldn't get caught up in sentimentality over something as stupid as Christmas. I don't like my employees weak."

"No, Markus, I agree." Lachlan's voice dripped with oily servitude. *The ultimate yes man.*

"Is that all?"

A pause. "No. Quinn has handed in her notice and will not be returning to her role at The Chimera."

A rage so intense that it blinded him twisted Markus in its grip. *That ungrateful upstart! Who does she think she is?* He stood abruptly, pushing the blonde away from him, sending the unfortunate woman sprawling on the plush carpet, her glass of champagne flying through the air in a graceful arc before landing in a puddle beside her.

"I don't want to hear her name again. You understand me?" Cold fury turned the words icy, ground from between clenched teeth.

"Yes, Markus. I'll have all mention of her removed from our systems before your return. I don't want to intrude anymore on your time. Merry Christmas again."

Markus stared at the phone in his hand for a moment before throwing it across the room in an explosion of rage, people ducking in panic out of its way. They turned bewildered gazes to him, gaping like a fish out of water, unsure what would sooth the beast that had been unleashed in him.

"Don't just stand there. Dance, you fools." Markus turned

to the disgruntled blonde who was drying her dress with a napkin. "And you, are you having fun yet? It's Christmas, after all." She nodded mutely. "Now, put a smile on your pretty face and go get me more Cristal. I don't keep you around for your personality."

LAS VEGAS, 8 MONTHS LATER

*P*resley smiled at the couple who had stopped talking to stare at her. From their badges, it appeared they were employees engaged in water cooler gossip rather than members of the public.

"Everything has been set up for you, and you will be residing in the palatial suite for your residency here with us at The Chimera." Kelly led the way through the VIP corridors, clearly having spent quite a bit of time in them judging from her familiarity. *Another place, another while to get used to its inner workings.* The life of a singer was one destined to be lived out of a suitcase, no matter how famous you became. "Mrs Barnett, would you and Presley like to meet with everyone first or settle in?"

Mrs Barnett, Presley's mother and manager, didn't break stride. "Let's get it over and done with so Presley can get to relaxin.'"

"If you'd like to come with me, I'll get everyone to meet us in the conference room," Kelly said, reaching for her two-way radio.

The conference room seemed to have been designed with a slightly male aesthetic with hard surfaces, sharp edges and glossy black everywhere. It screamed power and cold intimidation. It wasn't the first time Presley had been in a room that was meant to put the attendees ill at ease. Ten long years of clawing her way to the top of the country music pyramid and she'd seen her fair share of them. Heck, her mama thrived in them.

"They won't be too long," Kelly said once they were seated. "Can I get anything for you while we wait?"

"I'll have a tea," Mrs Barnett said. "I hope you remember how I like it."

Kelly grinned at the older woman, her eyes sparkling. "If y'all fixin' to bring me tea, better believe I want sweet tea, suga."

Presley was impressed. Kelly had done an outstanding job of mimicking her mother from their first meeting. She laughed. It was a relief to know that the PR and Marketing Manager and her mother were going to get along. After all, they were going to have to work closely together if they wanted her residency to be a success.

"Hush, child," her mother said, her mouth twitching.

"Yes, Mama."

"Presley, what would you like to have?" Kelly asked.

"Bloody Mary."

"Presley Barnett," her mama remonstrated, "it's too early for that, and I know you weren't raised in no barn."

"Is it?" Presley made a pretense of looking out the window to see if the sun was up. "Fine, I guess you better make that two sweet teas, please." Curiously, she watched as people began to filter into the room while Kelly phoned in their drink requests. A large intimidating man, his hair closely cut in military style, fairly filled the doorframe as he stepped through it, a small, immaculately dressed man hot on his heels and seemingly frustrated that his arrival hadn't been first. The little man made his way straight to Presley and took her hand in his, holding it in slightly damp fingers.

"Miss Barnett, I'm Lachlan, The Chimera's manager. It is a pleasure to have you staying at my casino. I'll do everything in my power to make your residency here pleasurable and successful for both of us." Presley extracted her now slightly moist hand from his, curiously watching Kelly roll her eyes behind Lachlan's back.

"I thought it was Markus's casino." Kelly raised her brows at him. "Better be careful he doesn't hear you talk like that. I don't believe he likes to share."

Lachlan gave her a dirty glare of reproach. "I believe Markus would know that I care for the casino as if it was my own. Now, if you would care to sit, Presley—is it all right if I call you that?" She nodded. "And Mrs Barnett, may I call you—"

"Mrs Barnett is fine." Her mama didn't bother letting him finish and took her place beside her daughter.

Presley tried to keep her face straight, but clearly Kelly had little respect for the casino manager, continuing to roll her eyes over his pompous ways. "Presley, this is Nate"—she gestured to the man with the military bearing—"he's the head of security here and will oversee all security, not only for your performances, but for your personal safety as well."

Nate had worldly brown eyes. It was clear the man had seen a lot of things in his life and most of them were probably still classified. "Pleasure to be looking after you, ma'am."

There was a quiet competence in him that Presley found immensely reassuring. "Thank you for looking after me."

"I have briefed my staff, but tomorrow we will need to go over what your movements will be like in the coming days and finalize the security plan for your performances." Nate leaned back in his chair, dinner plate sized hands resting palm down on the glossy black tabletop.

"I'll be able to go over Presley's itinerary with you, and I have a few things of my own I want to discuss with you tomorrow as well," Mrs Barnett said. *Mama was a stickler for the details.*

"Now, this was just an informal meet and greet of all of the power players of The Chimera." Kelly smiled as a young lady set the glasses of sweet tea in front of her guests. "I wanted you to be able to put faces to names of the people who are going to help make your residency here the success it's going to be."

"I wouldn't say it was all of the power players," Lachlan interrupted, mouth pressed tightly together. "I'm sure Markus would consider himself the biggest one."

Presley looked between the frowning Kelly and the glaring little manager. "Who's Markus?"

"Markus is the owner of The Chimera," Lachlan smugly announced. "And he has asked me to send you his regrets that he wasn't able to meet you today. He's been delayed in Monaco. However, he will be back in a few days' time and looks forward to making your acquaintance at that time."

"Well then, now that we've cleared that up, unless anyone else has anything to add, I think our guests would like to settle into their suite." Kelly rose after the briefest pause, giving only the barest lip service to anyone being able to add anything. "Excellent, if you would like to come with me."

Presley stood, making sure she grabbed her sweet tea off the table. Sure, it wasn't a Bloody Mary, but they sure did make a good beverage. A couple of corridors and one private elevator ride later and Kelly was ushering them into their suite. No matter how high Presley's star had risen, she always appreciated the degree of luxury that was now offered to her.

This was no different. Stunning views over The Strip tantalized her through the floor-to-ceiling windows, the entire space she stood in light-filled and airy. *Yes, this was going to do quite nicely.*

"If everything is to your standards, I have to go and finalize some last-minute scheduling for our Christmas events. I hear there's going to be an exclusive one-off performance from a country megastar."

Presley couldn't resist laughing at the obvious reference to herself. "I thought you were fixin' to sprain a muscle in there with all your eye rolling."

"What can I say? Lachlan is a kiss up. It's disgusting the way he is when Markus is around, but he must really want to impress you with the level he amped it up to back there." Kelly gave another eye roll for emphasis, laughing self-depreciatory.

"He just about pitched a fit when you left Markus out," Mrs Barnett noted, opening doors and looking inside curiously.

"Well, if you think Lachlan is bad, wait till you meet Markus. The most polite way I can describe him is as a first-class jerk. The man's jerkiness is legendary around the world, I imagine." Kelly slapped her forehead. "I almost forgot, these were made for you by—and I quote—your number one fan." She led the way into the massive kitchen. On the counter was a four-tier cake stand filled to overflowing with a multitude of delicate desserts.

"Oh my. I'm putting on weight just looking at it," Presley breathed.

Kelly looked her up and down, one brow raised skeptically. "I doubt that's something you need to worry about."

"Are you fixin' to just stand there moaning about calories or are you going to make a plate for your mama?" Mrs Barnett demanded.

Presley complied, licking her fingers free of the sticky, sugary goodness. "Who did you say made this again?"

"Our pastry chef, Marie. You might be the superstar of country, but she's the superstar of sugar." Kelly was clearly proud of her chef's skills.

"I couldn't have said it better." Presley snuck a treat from her mother's plate before handing it over.

"I saw that, child."

"I never could get anything pass you."

"Now, let Kelly go and do what she needs to do so you and I can go over your schedule for the next few days."

"Yes, Mama."

Settling in on the sofa beside her mother, she folded her legs comfortably under herself and began to twirl the ends of her long chestnut hair around her finger. A nervous thrill danced about in her belly. This was a brand-new show they'd put together, and no matter how good they thought it was, until they got it before a live audience, there was no way to tell for sure. As her mother went over rehearsals, costume fittings and media scheduling, she breathed deeply, enjoying the nervous energy that filled her. When she harnessed it, she knew she could make magic happen on stage. She wouldn't just be a star. She'd be a supernova.

*H*er long chestnut hair had been pulled back into a messy bun on top of her head. Dressed in leggings and a crop top, she appeared diminutive on stage beside her dancers as they rehearsed. From where he stood in the upper reaches of the theater seating, Markus found himself unable to look away from her. Presley Barnett had that inexplainable presence that only superstars are born with—that unmistakable X factor. *If she is this magnetic now, sweating and with no makeup on, the crowds are going to be beside themselves when she's in full costume.* Markus liked it when an investment looked good to return a profit.

"Presley, I think you girls have that one wrapped up. Do you want to start with the next one or break for the day?" the producer asked through the speaker.

She turned to her dancers and appeared to be in discussion with them. *She's the star, she should be telling them what she wants.* Markus couldn't understand why she would seek the opinion of people who were solely there at her pleasure.

"Y'all can break for the day. I think we need to make a few changes to the next number before we rehearse it." Presley's voice was smooth like the finest aged scotch, her Tennessee twang only adding to its warmth. "Thank you for y'all patience today." She graciously waved before walking off the stage and into the wings.

It's time Presley Barnett meets the person footing her bill. A keen sense of anticipation added fuel to an already oversized ego as he strode down the aisle toward her dressing room.

An older version of Presley was fussing around her as Kelly stood to one side, going over notes for upcoming media appointments that had been arranged to promote the grand opening performance of her residency at The Chimera. Seeing the cool blonde nod at him and then return her attention to Presley like she was the only person in the room set his teeth on edge.

"I expect you to schedule dinner with me in there, too, Kelly." Presley swiveled in her makeup chair at his words. Large whisky-colored eyes set in a delicate oval face stared at him, the face that had graced a hundred magazine covers. He didn't miss the delicately arched brow that suggested she wasn't amused by his comment.

"I'm sorry, but who are you?" Markus narrowed his eyes at her. *How dare she speak so dismissively to me.*

"I'm Markus Jamison, and I own this building your sitting in."

"Well, bless your heart," the older woman said. "But I don't recollect anything in Presley's contract stating that she was obligated to have dinner with you."

"Most women wouldn't consider it an obligation." Markus glared at the woman. The nosey old busybody needed to mind her own business.

"Oh, suga, you're not pretty enough to talk like that," she countered.

Markus glared ferociously at Kelly, her mouth twitching suspiciously. "Who is this woman? I want her out of here."

Intense astonishment touched her pale face and her gaze swung from him to the meddling older woman and Presley. "Ah, Markus, this is Mrs Barnett. She's Presley's manager and mother. Mrs Barnett, I believe Markus already introduced himself."

Embarrassment quickly turned to anger. *How dare Kelly set him up like that. He wasn't going to forget it. Not by a long shot.* "Mrs Barnett, it appears that there was some sort of misunderstanding of which I can only blame Kelly for not sufficiently informing me of who you were. However, my earlier request stands to have dinner with Presley." His voice was courteous, albeit patronizing. No longer willing to waste further effort on the mother, he turned to smirk at Presley. *If the girl was smart, she'd know that it wasn't an opportunity to squander.*

She really did have the most extraordinary eyes, the light brown flecked and ringed in gold. Obviously flattered by the attention he was showing her, she wet her lush mouth, complete with cupid's bow, with the tip of her tongue.

"Well, God love you." Presley's hand went to her heart, guilelessly smiling at him. "Because he's the only one who can." Markus blinked, startled at the abrupt deviation to what he'd anticipated her saying. "After the fit you just pitched at my mama, you're barking up the wrong tree if you think I would ever have dinner with someone so lacking in manners. Either that, or you're slower than molasses." Presley looked past him to Kelly. "Now, I believe I'm required for a final costume fitting. Is that right, Kelly?"

"Yes, Presley, if you'd like to come with me." Kelly didn't even bother to hide her amused enjoyment at the harsh take-down Markus had just been on the receiving end of as she led the way out of the room.

Not sparing him another moment of her attention and her vexation evident, Presley sailed from the room, leaving

Markus stupefied with what had just transpired. Stupefied, and seething with annoyance at the country singer's high-handed retort. *Just wait. Soon she'll be begging me, and then she'll regret how she just treated me.*

❧

THERE WAS SOMETHING ABOUT TASSELS, spangle and sequins that just set a girl's heart aflutter. A large part of the budget for her residency had been splurged on the fabulous costumes that she was now trying on. And because she didn't do thing by halves, she'd ordered a whole new set to be designed for her one-off Christmas concert as well. The dresser gave a final tug, pulling the waistline of the dress in tighter.

"What do you think?" she muttered around a mouthful of pins.

"I think I still need to be able to breathe." Presley tried to fill her lungs, testing the limits of the seams.

"Hush, child. No one said looking good on stage was comfortable—or practical, for that matter." Mrs Barnett's eyes narrowed as she swept the completed look with a practiced eye. "Under the lights, every move you make will dazzle. You might even wear it better than I did."

The costume Presley was currently pinned into was a modern take on one her mother had worn when she'd been the reigning Queen of Country before she'd made her family her focus. The top half of the dress was made to look like a western shirt with a wide yoke over the shoulders and buttons that went down the front. Spangled fringing dangled from under her sleeves like disco bat wings. The skirt stopped at mid-thigh, more tassels forming a fringe that hung from the hemline of the skirt, extending it down to below her knees. A large black rhinestone covered belt cinched her waist into tiny proportions. All she needed was to add the cowboy boots and she was ready to strut her stuff on stage.

"You must spend a fortune on rhinestone," Kelly marveled. "Now that I think about it, a star has to shine. I just never thought how to make that happen." She pretended to shield her eyes from the brightness.

Presley giggled and gave an extra wiggle, setting all the spangle to dancing about her. She loved the feeling of the movement against her skin and the rustle it made. It sent her nerves tingling, ready to perform, completely and totally alive. "If everyone's given this their approval, I'm going to change. That was the last one, wasn't it, Mama?"

"Yes." Her mother glanced down at her watch, a wrinkle forming between her brow. "And not a moment too soon. My shows are about to start. Quit fussing with your costume, child, and take it off. I'm fixin' to go up and spend some quality time on the sofa."

"If you don't have any plans, Presley, I was thinking I might go have a cocktail before I head upstairs." Kelly's suggestion sounded a heck of a lot more fun than watching Mama's soaps.

"That sounds great." Presley waited patiently while her dresser unzipped the back of her outfit. All stage costumes needed to be designed with quick fastenings to enable fast side-of-stage changes. A quick shimmy and it dropped from her shoulders and she was able to step out of it. Spangles and sequins were nice and all, but it sure did make an outfit heavy. With years of experience in fast wardrobe changes, Presley was ready in no time and following Kelly into a cock-tail bar.

"Can I please get a blue Hawaiian and whatever my friend would like."

Presley's eyebrows shot up. "That's not the drink I expected you to order. Isn't it a little old fashioned?"

"I have a soft spot for it, and sometimes old fashioned just means they've stood the test of time. Now, give the man your order, otherwise I might perish from thirst before I get my drink."

"Okay, keep your britches on. Can you make it two Hawaiians?"

"What happened to it being old fashioned?" There were traces of laughter in Kelly's voice. "Anyway, I thought you were more of a Bloody Mary kinda girl."

"Never let it be said that Presley Barnett isn't open to new experiences." She followed Kelly to a corner booth that offered a bit more privacy. "Thanks for asking me to come. I don't really get invited to many things."

"I find that hard to believe. I'm pretty sure everyone wants to hang out with you."

It was hard to explain the loneliness that was part of her job. Everyone felt like they knew her, but no one made the effort to just be a friend. "Um, well I get invited to things all the time, but I don't get asked to just hang out with girl-friends, if you know what I mean."

"Does that mean we're besties now? Cause I'm totally taking it if you are." Kelly smiled her thanks at the waitress delivering their cocktails. "I mean, I'll have to make sure Quinn is okay to share, but she's busy with Jackson at the moment anyway."

Presley couldn't help herself. She began to giggle, the Aussie's good nature infectious. She took a sip from the straw sticking out of the exceptionally tall glass. "Hmm, this is the best blue drink I've ever had. Maybe I should add it to my drinks repertoire."

Kelly closed her eyes blissfully as she sampled her own beverage. "You totally should. I've been meaning to thank you for donating an exclusive experience with you as a prize for Wyatt's charity auction. It raised a lot of money."

"I was happy to help. I'm surprised that Markus allowed you to offer it in his casino." Images of icy crystal blue eyes piercing into her made her shiver. "He doesn't exactly seem like the warm fuzzy kind."

"What can I say? The man's a jerk. Which is why it was easier to ask for forgiveness rather than permission. I might not have told him yet." Kelly's eyes sparkled mischievously. "I'm sure to get around to it eventually. Like, the day it happens."

"Oh, you're going to get me in so much trouble."

"Only the best kinds. Anyway, there are a lot of safe and happy horses that Markus unknowingly helped. Maybe just think of it like I'm helping him get some karma points and he doesn't even know it."

"Is it hard being away from your boyfriend?" Presley's last relationship had broken up when she'd realized it had been six months since they'd last been in the same city. *Guess that's what happens when you're both country singers.*

"Yeah, it is. That's why I'm about to hand my notice in. But I wanted to make sure you were settled before I did."

Presley smiled, careful to hide any traces of sadness. It wasn't like she wasn't used to being lonely, but somehow, with the residency this time, she'd hoped that she might actually make some friends. "I appreciate it. Now, tell me all about your man and this ranch of his."

Kelly's pale face seemed to glow, giving her an ethereal appearance. "Well, one of the first horses I ever met there, I'm now lucky enough to call my heart horse. His name's Maximus, and he's the biggest gentle giant I've ever met." She pulled out her phone. "Here's a picture from the first day I ever sat on him. It was like sitting on a barrel. He was that wide."

As the blonde girl talked, Presley wondered if, once Kelly was gone, she would be left to deal with the black-haired casino owner. There was something about him that was at once both appealing and repellent. His features were hand-some—the square jaw, striking pale blue eyes, the dark slashes of his brows, the lush mouth. But there was a sullen-ness that cast a shadow over everything. Those same eyes were cold and hard, the mouth pressed into a petulant pout, the jaw set into an unforgiving line. She knew she could hold her own with him, but maybe it was best to not cause herself grief and just avoid him. *How hard could it be? It was only his casino, after all.*

"Oh my gosh, PRESLEY!" screeched the pretty girl with rainbow-colored hair, throwing her arms wide as she ran toward her.

"Suzie, wow, your hair is really something else." Presley laughed as she jumped up and down with her in the dressing room.

Suzie let her go and touched the ends of her kaleidoscope tresses, giggling. "I just finished working on a film in Istanbul, it was very noir." She waggled her eyebrows dramatically. "And somehow this seemed like the best way to celebrate its completion."

"Well, not many people could pull it off, but you have certainly managed to." Presley put down the song setlist she'd been reading. "And you've managed to time it brilliantly. I'm finished for the day. Have you checked in to your accommodation yet?"

"Yeah, I'm sharing with two of your dancers. It's pretty nice and even has a pool. And yes, there will be pool parties in our future."

Suddenly Presley wasn't feeling so lonely after all. She

linked her arm with Suzie's. "If you've got time, I know Mama would love to say hello."

"You know I've always got time for Mrs Barnett. Plus, I bet she's got a list a mile long waiting for me." Suzie settled into stride with Presley following her out into the corridor.

"It's like you've met my mother before." Presley laughed.

"A time or two."

"What's the deal with Rainbow Brite?" Presley's stomach clenched at the condescending voice that echoed down the hall, his words loaded with ridicule.

"Just ignore him. Maybe if we do it long enough, he'll disappear," Presley muttered to Suzie.

"Who is he?" Suzie whispered back, casting quick glances at Markus from lowered lashes as they got closer. She fairly hummed with vivid curiosity.

"Are you going to tell me who Skittles is or not?" His mocking tones irked her, and despite her best intentions to ignore him, Presley found herself rounding on him.

"Suzie is my friend, and that means you'll treat her with respect."

"If she wants respect, then I suggest she doesn't make fashion choices that make her look like a Care Bear vomited on her." Gosh she wanted to wipe that patronizing smirk right off his dang face.

It didn't help that Suzie began to giggle hysterically. "Whoever he is, he's a riot."

Markus raised one dark brow sardonically at the chuckling Suzie. "I own this casino."

"Well, good for you. I like seeing people do well in life," Suzie congratulated him, wiping at her eyes.

Markus seemed at a momentary loss for words as though unsure how to take her comment. Apparently, his default setting was smug and overbearing. "I expect you to be ready for dinner at eight."

"Excuse me?" *That's it, he's going down a peg or two now.*

"You need to have made yourself suitably presentable by eight for dinner." Each word was emphasized like he was talking to a child. Suzie made a funny choking, hiccupping sound beside her, eyes wide to gauge her reaction to Markus's obnoxious, high-handed attitude.

Presley raised a brow, lifting her chin to better look down her nose at him. No small feat given their height difference. "Are things done differently here?"

"I presume lots of people have dinner at eight," he drawled with distinct mockery.

"Well, where I'm from, you ask a lady, not snap your fingers and expect her to obey. And make no mistake, I'm a lady through and through." Smiling sweetly at him, she linked her arm with Suzie's again and merrily left him to stew in his own juices. *Take that, Mr High and Mighty. You're playing with a southern gal now.*

THE CRYSTAL TUMBLER'S edges dug into his palm as Markus stared out over The Strip. *Who did she think she was, talking to him like he was no one?* But with that thought came grudging respect. She knew exactly who she was. She was Presley Barnett, country superstar, beloved by the masses. Quite simply, she was one of the most famous people on the planet and she had no intentions of making things easy for him. And easy for him would be if he could make himself stay away from her. Markus clenched his mouth tighter. This time he was determined to keep his distance. The increase of his heart rate at the thought put lie to his intentions.

"Oh, goody. You're here," Kelly said sarcastically, striding into his office.

"Go away."

"Will do. Just need to give you this." She dropped a piece of paper on his desk and, without bothering to wait for an answer, turned to leave.

"What is it?" Kelly usually emailed all correspondence she had for him.

"I thought you didn't want to know?"

Markus turned to glare at her. He'd just about had it with smart-mouthed women today. "What is it?" he ground out.

"It's my notice. I'm resigning." He was convinced that she only smiled at him to further goad his temper.

"I'll get Lachlan started on finding your replacement immediately. The sooner we have one, the sooner I don't have to see your face again." Markus drained the last of the scotch.

Kelly laughed, completely unfazed by his vitriol. "The feeling is one hundred percent mutual. But that aside, I'll still have to give a handover to my successor. Anyway, other things to do and all that." Whistling cheerfully, she waltzed from the room. Drawing on a strength of willpower he was surprised he possessed, he managed to refrain from throwing his glass at the door. Instead he satisfied himself with stabbing angrily at his phone.

"Lachlan, I want you to find me a new PR and Marketing Manager. And this time I want a man. Someone I can work with."

Throwing the phone down hard on the desk, he stalked from the room. He needed to take a drive in one of his sportscars—maybe the Bugatti. The open road and some speed were what he needed to blow his women troubles away once and for all. A pair of whisky eyes taunted him from his mind. Somehow, he doubted even his supercar had the speed required to make that a reality.

CHAPTER 5

The man standing beside Kelly in the wings of the stage looked a little shellshocked by all the activity around him. He had a large, round, rather nondescript face with a pleasant expression. Presley wiped the sweat from her face as she strolled over, her muscles fatigued from the day's rehearsal.

"Presley, this is Paul Lawrence. He's going to be replacing me as the PR and Marketing Manager," Kelly introduced them.

"Kelly is getting me up to speed on what she's done and what's left to be completed. I'm sure we'll be able to transition smoothly and with minimal disruption." Paul's face split into a wide grin, his eyes wide with excitement. Presley found herself smiling back at his enthusiasm—fans often had that reaction—till she realized his attention was fixed on a point over her shoulder. "Wilma Barnett, it's an honor." He pushed past, Presley forgotten in his haste. Kelly looked just as disgruntled as Presley felt as they stared at each other. *What on God's green earth?*

"Suga, have we met?" Mrs Barnett looked over at the girls and hesitated, blinking with bafflement.

"No, but I've been a big fan for a long time." Paul was the picture of eager adoration.

Mrs Barnett's hand went to her necklace, toying with the pearls. "As I live and breathe, a fan. Suga, you don't look old enough to know who I am."

Kelly shrugged helplessly at Presley, making a face. "Mrs Barnett, this fan, I mean Paul"—she gave him a hard look, very clearly telling him to get it together because he was embarrassing her—"is the new PR and Marketing Manager."

Mrs Barnett held out her hand. "Well then, suga, it looks like we're fixin' to be seeing more of each other."

Paul's hand shook slightly as he clasped hers. *I wonder if his palms are all sweaty.* With what appeared to be intense willpower, he managed to return to being a professional. Presley was honestly impressed with how he morphed between the two demeanors. Kelly obviously wasn't willing to risk a repeat performance.

"Paul and I have a few more things to go over before the meeting. We'll see you both there." She leveled a hard look at Paul, a brow cocked. "Well, I'll be there at least."

"He seemed nice." Mrs Barnett picked up a cowboy hat that had been discarded by a careless dancer. "I'll have to have another word with the crew about looking after the props."

Presley regarded her mother with amusement. Mama had definitely enjoyed the attention Paul had shown her. She held her hand to her chest. "Well, hello, suga. Do I need to tell Daddy?"

"Hush, child, and your daddy knows I love him." Her mother cast a critical eye over her. "Have you eaten yet?"

"No. I was fixin' to grab something after I had a shower to clean up."

"Well, stop giving cheek to your mama and get upstairs. I'll call for some lunch on my way up."

Presley wrapped her arms around her mother. "I do love you."

Mrs Barnett gave her a fierce hug. "I love you, too." She wrinkled her nose. "Now go shower. You smell."

After freshening up and having a quick bite to eat, with a rapidness that made her head whirl, she went from having her mind focused as a performer to that of a businesswoman sitting in a boardroom. She'd been in this room several times and each visit left her feeling like she was an interloper to a male domain. It struck her as curious the seats people took, how close they wanted to be to the power. At the head of the table, Markus looked down like a great medieval lord. Lachlan, she noticed, always took the position to his immediate right. Kelly always left a space between her and Markus. Today it was filled by Paul. Presley couldn't be sure whether or not it had been by design by the new employee. Nate took whichever seat was free, the man quietly confident enough not to be drawn into any power struggles. Presley took her own place beside Kelly. *Us gals have to stick together, after all.* Her mother elected to sit next to her.

Markus's lips twisted into a cynical smile. "Tell me how you're going to make me money." He waved his hand about. "Kelly, you can start. Oh wait, you're not going to be working for me much longer. Paul, you're up." Kelly sent him a filthy glare.

Paul's Adam's apple bobbed as he swallowed, flustered to find himself suddenly on the spot. *The poor man. Why does Markus have to be such a jerk to people?* "Well, it's still early days of my handover, so hopefully I don't make too much of a meal of this." His gaze flickered around the assembled managers.

"Your job depends on you not." Markus's bored voice was heavy with threat.

Presley could see Kelly roll her eyes, and she was inclined to agree with her sentiments. *What was with the power trip Markus was always on?*

"In the coming days, Presley will be having her final dress rehearsal. Media and influencers have been invited to attend to garner reviews. She will also be doing a round of media commitments to promote the grand opening of her residency here at The Chimera."

"I know the name of my own hotel," Markus drawled sarcastically. Paul perceptively flinched at his tone. "Kelly, I expect you to have him fully across his role before you leave." Kelly gave a mocking salute in response.

"Nate, have the plans for security around Presley been finalized?"

The large, somber-faced man nodded. "I've rotated my best men to be responsible for security around the entrances to the theater and also access to backstage. A new security camera system upgrade was also implemented prior to her arrival. Everyone who enters the backstage area will have to pass security and swipe to gain access." He smiled reassuringly at Presley, showing large white teeth. "No one is getting in or out that I won't know about."

Markus nodded approvingly. It appeared that even the haughty, smug casino owner knew better than to tangle with the grizzled veteran. He lounged casually back against his chair. "I have complete faith in your ability to keep our star safe." Presley jolted at the strangely intimate way he said *our star.* "Lachlan, is there anything else you wish to discuss?"

"I think they've covered everything, sir." The casino manager smiled fawningly at him. Without even looking at Kelly, Presley knew she'd be doing another one of her infamous eye rolls.

"Meeting is over then. Get back to work, everyone, and make me more money." Markus's black hair gleamed under the light. Steepling his fingers together, he tapped his mouth gently with his index fingers. "Presley, I have a dinner tonight that I require you to attend."

She rose fluidly from her chair, her sweet smile betraying none of her annoyance. "You'll need to discuss that with my manager."

"Presley has prior commitments for tonight." Dear Mama could always be relied on to handle a situation.

"Cancel them." Markus's eyes went flat at her refusal.

"Bless your heart, I'm real torn up by it, but it's just not possible." Mrs Barnett made a show of looking at her watch. "We best be going if we're fixin' to make it on time." She shooed Presley out the door like a bustling mother hen.

"Mama, we don't really have anything on tonight, do we?" Presley whispered. Her mother had, after all, been very convincing.

"Only with my soaps and a big plate of chicken and waffles."

Presley laughed. "Well ain't no way I'm fixin' on canceling that."

THE NEXT FEW days were once again a whirl of engagements, speaking to bloggers and podcasts, and interviews with entertainment channels. After a grueling day spent doing back-to-back radio interviews, Presley settled back into the plush leather seats of the limo absolutely spent. Wanly, she smiled at her mama as she handed Presley a thermos filled with hot water, honey and lemon.

"Thanks, Mama." Her voice was husky from overuse.

"Hush, child. Rest your voice."

"Paul, I've locked in all the media for our Christmas events except for a few things left to finalize for Presley's Christmas concert, but I'm sure you'll be able to handle those last-minute things. Don't worry about Markus. If you need help with anything, you will still be able to call me once I'm gone." Kelly was on the final countdown to finishing up and washing her hands of the casino. Presley suspected most of her obvious eagerness had to do with escaping the jerk who owned it. So far, Presley had managed to avoid him, but she knew her days were numbered.

"I'll make sure Presley is well taken care of, Kelly, and I appreciate your offer. No matter what Markus says, I'll make sure she gets the level of care and attention that a star of her caliber deserves." Presley smiled in thanks at Paul. He really was the sweetest man.

"After the Christmas concert, you won't have to worry about me for a few weeks. We're headed back to the family farm in Franklin for Christmas and fixin' to stay there till my New Year's Eve concert." Presley sipped her tea, her scratchy throat immediately soothed by the warm liquid. "My voice will need a break by then anyway."

"It's my job to worry about you," Paul said, his kind eyes earnest.

"And I'll try not to give you too much to worry about," she pledged in return. The water in her cup sloshed about as the car pulled to a halt, her mother quickly getting a Kleenex ready just in case of spillage. "It's okay, Mama. I managed to save it."

She alighted from the car, enjoying the warmth of the sun on her face as she stepped out. It was coming into the time of the year where the long shadows cast by the casinos lining The Strip could leave a body cold. It had been a rarity in the last few days as she'd been shuttled from casino to limo to studio, rinse and repeat, that she'd felt the sun's gentle caress. It was something to savor. She closed her eyes blissfully.

THE SUNLIGHT SENT ripples of caramel and fire through her gleaming chestnut hair as she lifted her face, seeking the sun's kiss. Markus stood in the foyer waiting for his car to be brought around. These days, he found he was more in need than ever of the solitude from his thoughts that the powerful vehicle provided. Every day, he would see her swanning around with her entourage, laughing and shining brightly as if lit from within. And every time, he vowed that next time he would be able to resist her siren song. That underneath all the fame and fortune she was just like any other woman he'd ever met—easily forgotten.

The lies we tell ourselves. But he was a gambler and always would be. A lie is only a lie until you believe it, and then you can sell it as the truth. One dinner was all it would take, and then the mystique that he'd built up around her would tarnish and she would be just like the rest. *One dinner*, he vowed, stalking to his waiting car.

THE POLISHED WOOD was cool against his knuckles as he knocked. The corridor he stood in was eerily still, the air smelling artificially sweet. Surprise rocked him when Presley answered the door herself. There was no way Markus would lower himself to do so. It's why he had a butler. Heck, it's why they'd provided her with a butler, too.

"Where's Jonathon?" he demanded.

"Well, hello to you, too. And if you mean Jonathon, the butler, he was reassigned to the high roller suite, I believe.

But you'd have to check with your staff." She smiled benignly like one would to a wayward child.

He could hear laughter coming from her room, a low male rumble amongst it. Jealousy twisted in his gut. "Why was he reassigned?"

"I don't need a butler. I prefer privacy." *To entertain that man in your room.* The unwanted vision twisted in his mind. "Now, my turn for questions. What do you want, Markus?" Delicately arched brows were raised in challenge as she peered at him.

"Will you have dinner with me tonight?" He schooled his expression into one of complete unconcern. "There, I even asked."

She laughed, the hardness around her eyes softening. "Yes, you did. But I'm busy tonight."

"Of course. I can hear you have other plans," he bit out. Humiliated that he'd lowered himself to grovel only to be refused, he went to turn on his heel.

"Markus." She said his name gently, soft upon her lips, and he was powerless to leave. She swung the door open wider to reveal Kelly, Marie, Suzie, Paul, Nate—*really, Nate, too?*—and Mrs Barnett clustered around a monopoly board. "Would you like to join us?"

"No, I can see you already have company. Goodnight, Presley." This time he strode away before he could weaken.

Soft as a sigh, "Goodnight, Markus" floated down the hall after him.

Soon after, he was standing alone, slowly shedding his clothes, surrounded by the cedar and dark wallpaper of his walk-in dressing room. Custom made suits hung according to color, a wall of handmade Italian shoes lined up neatly in their shelving. In the center, a cabinet held his watches and cufflinks, the drawers full of silk ties. Here, he felt safe, surrounded by his wealth. Here, he was impenetrable. Yet how had a pair of softly glowing, warm brown eyes left him feeling vulnerable to his core, and the thought of her with another man driving a spike of jealousy so deep into his soul that he still could feel fragments of it? Her gentle goodnight weakening his resolve that he'd almost turn, seeking to join his employees in their ghastly board game. *One dinner, and I'll forget her like the rest.*

CHAPTER 6

The air crackled with barely suppressed electricity. Everywhere people scurried about, some in various stages of undress as production staff secured mics, dressers made last-minute alterations, and stagehands moved equipment. Beyond the curtain, a restless murmuring of the crowd floated to Presley's ears. *Nothing like opening night to make you feel alive.*

Bob and Edna, the winners of the charity auction held for Kelly's boyfriend, hovered nearby with the Marketing Manager and her mama decked out in their custom fan shirts covered in printed photos of her. Their eyes darted every which way as they soaked in the alien atmosphere. Although thoroughly nice people, their adoration had quickly begun to feel cloying. The usual spiel of them being her number one fans had quickly disintegrated to them trying to impress her with facts about her, some quite random and obscure. A trickle of unease had rolled up her spine at the situation, and it had been a relief to smile graciously at them, promising to sing their favorite song when Mama had announced it was time for her to begin preparations for the show.

"It's a full house out there." Paul bounced on the balls of his feet as he peered at her, trying to gauge her level of nerves. "Are you excited?"

Presley closed her eyes and inhaled all the air she could, filling her lungs till they were fit to burst, slowly releasing her pent-up breath. "I feel alive. My blood is coursing through my veins, every nerve tingling in anticipation."

His eyes studied hers with a curious intensity, a gleam of interest shining. It seemed at odds with his blandly, pleasant features.

"I need to turn on your mic pack." Presley turned her back to comply and when she looked back at Paul, his expression was his normal affable self again.

Kelly bustled the fans over, Mama with them. "Presley, I'm going to take Bob and Edna to get their seats now."

She smiled at them, rapturous worship staring back at her. "It was great meeting y'all. Thank you so much for helping out the charity. Now, remember I'm fixin' to sing your song for you." Another quick photo op and Kelly was shooing them away, casting an apologetic grimace over her shoulder.

"Did you make sure you had your honey?" Mama asked, adjusting the collar of her denim jacket.

"Yes, Mama," Presley responded as was expected as part of their pre-performance ritual.

"Been to the bathroom?"

"Yes, Mama."

Her mother held out a water bottle. "Have a drink." Presley took a swig from the proffered bottle. "I love you. Now, go give these people the show of their lives."

Presley grinned, knowing her eyes would be sparkling, fierce with excitement. "Yes, Mama." Head high and shoulders thrust back, she strutted into the familiar heat of the spotlight, the thunderous roar of the crowd sweet to her ears. *Showtime.*

SHE OVERWHELMED MARKUS'S SENSES. A dazzling spectacle, shining so bright that he would have turned away if he'd been able to. Country music wasn't really his thing, and he sure as heck had never had a hankering to attend a concert in his own casino before. Somehow Presley Barnett made him want to do things he normally wouldn't. *That's a dangerous power to give someone, especially a woman.* Even where he stood in the front row, a barricade between him and the great unwashed masses, the passion, the hunger of the crowd for her was palpable. It might have had something to do with how, in the way she greeted the audience, it felt like each word was directed at you, a dear friend of hers. Markus cast a dark look at the couple beside him, making a mental note to talk to Nate about tightening the security if people like that managed to get into the platinum VIP area.

He gave a shiver of distaste, taking in the homemade signs and T-shirts that looked like they'd been printed on their home computer. *What is that, anyway?* Markus curled his lip in derision when he realized they were pictures of Presley. *Too cheap to even buy official merchandise.*

The music started, the crowd's restless energy buffeting him about, and then she lifted her face, washed out under the spotlights. Her glorious voice wrapped itself around Markus, turning him inside out, intoxicating and addictive. *I swear she's singing to me.* Wide eyed, he was lost to her siren song.

SHE SHOULD BE SPENT. Every ounce of her energy had been left on the stage and yet, as it had been since the first time she'd stepped onstage at one of her mama's concerts, she was buzzing, her nerves humming. Paul was waiting with Mrs Barnett and Kelly, ready to hustle her daughter to the sanctuary of the dressing room. But even there she could feel the presence of others.

The low coffee table and her makeup area were strewn with flowers, gifts and cards. "And I thought I got some sweet gifts in my job," marveled Kelly, taking it all in. She stooped to pick up an enormous bouquet of the most amazing flowers Presley had ever seen. Presley had been on the receiving end of more than one floral arrangement in her life, but she couldn't identify what they were.

"This is a little job-well-done-on-your-first-show present from The Chimera."

Presley accepted, breathing in a musty dry smell mingled with eucalyptus. "I doubt Markus picked these for me."

Kelly grinned wickedly at her, large eyes guileless. "Oh, silly me, when I said 'The Chimera', I meant they paid for it, I picked them."

"Well, thank y'all. What kind are they? I've never seen anything like them before."

"Grevillea and protea flowers, and the silvery colored foliage are juvenile eucalyptus leaves. I can't remember what those little pompom looking flowers are called."

Mrs Barnett took the flowers from Presley. "I'll find a vase for these."

Presley looked at the spread of confectionary and cakes on the table and held her hands to her waist in mock protest. "I'm beginning to think Marie is trying to fatten me up."

"Or sweeten you up," Mrs Barnett added from the other side of the room.

"Nothing could make her sweeter." Paul blushed as if suddenly realizing he'd spoken the words aloud.

Presley giggled. "Thanks, Paul, but Mama might disagree with you there. Marie told me the other day that she wants to go back to her hometown and open a dessert bar one day."

"The girl has talent. Maybe it would be a waste for her to hide it in some small town. She'd make more money headlining as the pastry chef in a big hotel or casino like here," Mrs Barnett disagreed. *Trust Mama, always with one eye to business.*

"Maybe it isn't about the money for her. Maybe it's about using her talent and passion in a way that feeds her soul. Speaking of which." Presley plucked a caramel tart from the display. "Yep, that's feeding my soul right there," she said around a mouthful of gooiness, crumbs falling out. "If she opened one, I'd sure as heck make sure I was there for the grand opening."

Mrs Barnett bustled back. "I think it's time Presley got out of her costume before she gets food all over it." She shooed everyone from the room, the sudden quiet jolting.

Idly, Presley looked over the other gifts on the table. Some from radio stations she'd done interviews for, a bunch of daisies, bright and happy, but with no card to identify their sender and a small blue box tied with a white ribbon. Curious, she picked it up, gently untying it, the top of the box lifting off easily. Inside lay delicately wrought platinum and diamond drop earrings shaped to look like trailing vines. *He has exquisite taste.* Presley wasn't sure how she knew they were from Markus, but she did even before she extracted the pristinely white card from the envelope secured inside the box.

Have dinner with me?

M

She turned the card over in her hands. The gift felt

somehow intimate. *Oh, who am I kidding? He probably got his assistant to purchase them—and the flowers-with-no-name, for that matter.* Presley blew out her cheeks, considering Markus's request. He'd asked once before, and she'd turned him down. This time, maybe it was time to say yes.

A quick change and then, securely wedged between Paul and her mama, Kelly leading the way and a vigilant Nate escorting them, Presley made her way out of the stage door. A throng of people were waiting, eagerly holding up programs and merchandise, camera phones flashing to get a picture. Taking a camera from a fan, she handed it to Paul.

"Can you take a photo?" Presley leaned in close till her cheek was pressed against the woman's, smiling brightly until the flash made her stand up tall again.

"Presley, do you think it's wise to stop here?" Nate anxiously scanned the crowd.

"Nate, this is something I do after every performance. Without my fans, I wouldn't even be doing a show here." Presley leaned in for another selfie with a fan.

"You only do them while I say it's safe to do them," he grumbled, clearly unhappy with her decision.

"Suga, I'll do them while people still want them and until the last fan leaves." Turning her back on his frowning face, she signed a program. "And then I'll probably do one more."

"THEY SUIT YOU." Markus waved a manicured finger at her ear lobes. "Their beauty dazzles." His eyes drank in the vision before him. Unsettled, he picked up his wine glass. "I must admit, I'm surprised you finally accepted a dinner invitation from me. Does this mean I'm starting to grow on you?"

"Like mold." Presley smiled sweetly at him, toying with

her fork. "I figured you were just playing a percentages game with me. At some point, the odds had to be in your favor."

A ripple of amusement went through him. What had goaded him to the point of fury or, at the very least, passionate dislike in other women had somehow garnered his respect with this woman. Her feistiness added to his attraction for her. "I'll admit that I thought I would have to play a long game."

"But where are my manners? Thank you for the gift. I kinda suspected your assistant picked them out." She peeked at him adorably from behind lowered dark eyelashes across the other side of the table. He found himself wishing he'd picked a smaller one.

Markus had never seen anything so adorable in his life. *Stop it. Markus Jamison does not do adorable. He does hot, he does beautiful, and he does disposable.* "I selected them for you, however my assistant organized them." He spread his hands wide. "I am, after all, a busy man."

"Yes, what is it that you do again, international man of gambling?" There was something warm and enchanting in her humor.

"Don't forget that I own this casino." He picked at a non-existent spot on the pristine tablecloth.

There was a teasing laughter in her eye. "You don't let anyone forget. Me, I'm just a simple gal from Tennessee out here singing a few songs."

"Presley Barnett, there's nothing simple about you." Markus snapped his mouth shut, clenching it tightly together to prevent any further words from escaping. *I sound like a gushing fool. Stick with the plan. One dinner, and then she won't fascinate me anymore and I'll lose interest. Just like all the others.*

"Suga, you're saying the nicest things tonight. Bless you, are you dying?" The casual way she threw his life around caught him off guard. *That, and being called suga.*

"I'm shocked at you. I thought nice southern girls wouldn't joke about someone's life like that."

Presley set her glass back on the table, molten bronze eyes suddenly serious. "I am. I always try to find the best in people, and you're not exactly the easiest to find the best in."

Markus's stomach hardened, the truth bitter to hear. *It's not like it has ever mattered before.* "I think you're a fool. If you expect the worst from people, you're very rarely disappointed."

He looked away from the pity on her face. "That's a horrible way to live, always on guard. Who hurt you to make you like that?"

Her eyes seemed to penetrate straight to his soul. Uncomfortably, he shifted in his seat. "I hear you have a Christmas concert coming up."

Presley gave him a level look, a probing inquiry in her keen eyes. "Yes, a one-off for my last performance before I head home for a break over Christmas." Thankfully, it appeared she was willing to let it go. *If she'd pushed, would I have told her?* The thought of being vulnerable had his mind shuddering. "I love Christmas, so starting to celebrate it early is just the best thing. And it's nice to share some of that holiday spirit with my fans." She raised a brow at him. "I'm going to go out on a limb here and take a wild stab in the dark." Presley waved her wineglass at him. "Christmas is totally your thing. In fact, you're known for your fabulous collection of holiday sweaters."

Markus almost choked on his mouthful of wine. Trying to salvage the situation, he covered his coughing with his napkin. "Hardly. I hate it. Actually, that's not true." A glimmer of surprise shone across her face. "Christmas makes me a lot of money, and I do like making money. So we both look forward to something at Christmas." Markus enjoyed the look of outraged betrayal that chased the hope from her face just a little too much.

"Is it always about winning with you?" Her tone was coolly disapproving.

He raised his glass to her in mock salute. "Is there anything else?" The problem was, he was beginning to think there might be.

A week into Presley's residency and it already felt like home. She owed a large part of that to the careful preparations that had taken place, the attention to detail that Kelly had devoted to making her time at The Chimera not only hugely successful but also comfortable. The fact she'd found a friend in the process was something she would cherish for the rest of her life. All around conversation swirled and glasses clinked. Below Presley could see people gathered in groups, women teetering on high heels and men in tight-fitting shirts. From time to time, someone would point toward the cordoned off VIP lounge, eyes speculative. Kelly, walking back from the bathroom, said something in passing to Suzie, leaving her laughing.

Presley couldn't help but feel an intense sense of loss. Today was Kelly's farewell drinks. In this industry, people came and went, but friends were to be treated as the rare treasure that they were. As if sensing her gaze upon her, Kelly turned and waved cheerfully, complete contentment with the world radiating from her as she made her way over.

Presley was overcome with guilt for her melancholy. *How selfish am I?*

Kelly slid gracefully onto the black leather sofa beside her. "Why so glum, chum?"

"I'm going to miss you." Presley really wished it hadn't come out sounding so whiny.

The Aussie put an arm around her. "Aw, come here." She pulled her in close. "I've dealt with a lot of famous people." Kelly released her to do air quotes. *Wow, she must have had a bit to drink if she's using those.* "And you are, without a doubt, my favorite one. And you're the real deal." Presley opened her mouth to return the sentiment, coming up short when Kelly held up her index finger to indicate she still had more to say as she took a drink. Presley giggled at the sight of the familiar blue cocktail. "I don't make friends easily. In fact, I only really have one friend."

"Quinn," Presley said as casually as she could manage, beginning to feel the sting of rejection.

"Yep, Quinn. And I might be overstepping here, but I'd like to add you to that list."

Presley couldn't stop the grin if she tried. "Y'all won't be able to get rid of me. Have you told Quinn?'

"Yep. She said to ask if you wanted to come visit for Christmas."

"Oh, I can't." Presley was crestfallen. "I already have plans for this year."

"I told her that I thought it might be short notice, but I still wanted to ask. Now, for what it's worth, I know you're in safe hands with Paul looking after you. He's got everything under control. Seriously, some days he knew more about what you were doing than I did, and I made the arrangements. He promised me that you will be his focus. He wants everything to be perfect for you." Kelly leaned in a little closer, blinking owlishly. "I mean, I even have everything locked in as far as marketing for your Christmas concert. You just need to work with Paul to confirm song list, costuming and stage sets."

Presley nodded, looking across to where Paul was deep in conversation with her mother. Whatever it was about seemed to involve a lot of arm waving and laughing. Suddenly she wished her daddy was there. It had been over a month since they'd last seen him. Unfortunately, he was caught up with his own commitments and hadn't been able to come this time. *Christmas can't come soon enough.* She continued to sweep the room with her gaze.

"Markus didn't come?'

Kelly gave an unladylike snort. "I didn't invite him."

"Kelly, you're being ugly."

"How can I put this delicately?" Kelly pursed her lips together thoughtfully. "He isn't my biggest fan, and I'm not his. Basically, he's a first-class jerk and I don't like him. But then again, I don't have to. I'm leaving, and I'm not the one who had dinner with him the other night." Her friend gave her a look that was just a little too knowing.

"I did, and he wasn't completely horrible to me."

Intense astonishment touched Kelly's pale face. "Are you saying he was actually nice?"

"I wouldn't go that far. But maybe his bark is worse than his bite." Presley gave a helpless shrug.

"Having worked for the man for over two years, I highly doubt it. But honestly, come tomorrow, I'll never need to see the man again. You have no idea how good it will be to not have to stress about The Chimera these holidays. No Christmas Eve phone calls, no Christmas Day emergencies. Just Wyatt, the horses and me. And a whole lot of Gregory's."

"That sounds a lot like what I'm looking forward to as well. My sister and brother and their families live near the farm, and I haven't seen them or my nieces and nephews for what feels like ages. And don't get me started on seeing my daddy."

Presley felt tears of homesickness burn her eyes. She missed her family. Everyone had sacrificed to give her the opportunities she had. When they were younger, her siblings had accepted that at least one parent would be traveling with her instead of always being together. And Mama had even given up her own recording career for her. Christmas was a time where she could give thanks to them for all of that and to be with the family she cherished so much.

"You're from Tennessee, aren't you?" Kelly asked. *Only an Aussie wouldn't be able to pick my accent.*

"Yep. Originally, we're from Nashville, but when I got my first big check, I bought the family farm just outside of it in a place called Franklin. It even has a tire rope swing that I can see from my recording studio and a stream. It's nice to have somewhere I can be with my horses and the rest of the animals and just breathe after living like"—she waved her hand around the nightclub—"this. Y'all have to come down and visit sometime."

"I'd love to." Kelly gave her a friendly nudge with her shoulder. "Now, can I interest you in adopting another horse for your farm?"

Presley grinned. "I'm not saying no."

Kelly returned her smile and, fumbling, pulled her phone from her pocket. "Let's start with Terrance. He's a lovely little fella and just needs a bit of a chance."

A warm glow chased away her sense of loss with the realization that Kelly was leaving The Chimera but would always be a part of her life. Strangely, her thoughts wandered to Markus. *Would he be the same?*

~

THERE WAS a happy little bounce to Markus's step as he made his way through the corridor of his casino. To be fair, it was a novel experience for him and one that he marveled at, much like one would a two-headed donkey … speaking mandarin. If Markus was completely honest with himself, and in the privacy of his own mind, he unfailingly was, he'd narrowed it down to two possible options. The departure of that thorn in his side, the pimple on his bottom, the splinter in his finger—Kelly. Or—and this was where he was headed into dangerous territory—the fact that absolutely delightful thoughts of Presley flitted through his mind. *Delightful? Since when did I start thinking like a schoolgirl?*

His scowl turned into a small smile at the fact that his feet had miraculously decided to take it upon themselves to deliver him to Presley's dressing room door. Not bothering to knock—the door was partially open anyway—he sauntered in. "Is it just my imagination or does the sky seem bluer since Kelly left?" he commented as if the answer was obvious. *Of course, it was since the Australian storm cloud had left.*

Presley glared at him in the reflection of her mirror while Suzie buzzed about doing her hair. *Like a bee buzzing around an exquisite flower.* Judging from her narrowed-eye glare, she wasn't amused. "Why are your words always so ugly?"

He opened his eyes innocently at her, at odds with the half smirk he knew played upon his lips. "Have you seen outside? It's a gorgeous day."

Presley spun around in her chair. *If she's not careful she's going to give herself whiplash.* "I'm sitting here torn up 'cause I miss my friend, and you talk about her leaving like it's the best thing that ever happened." Her extraordinary eyes blazed and glowed.

He retained his composure but he could feel the hardening of his eyes. "That's because, for me, never seeing Kelly again is better than beating the house in Monaco."

"There it is. Back to winning again," Presley retorted in cold sarcasm, turning back to allow Suzie to finish her hair, her vexation evident.

Markus frowned, his jacket pulling tight against his back as he huffily crossed his arms. *Where does she get off being all high and mighty?* "In the end, nothing else matters to me except winning." He hated how the flash of hurt in her reflected eyes stabbed at him, clawing into his gut. Why did he even care what she thought?

Presley stood and strolled closer, each stride fluid. Markus held his breath as she paused at his side, facing away from him, her light perfume making him think of sunshine and daisies. "In the end, y'all be alone." With stiff dignity, she left, leaving him feeling like the sun had gone out.

"Excuse me, sir." A stagehand stood hesitantly at the door.

"What is it?" he barked, the words harsh in the quiet room.

The teenager flinched, tentatively holding out an envelope. "I was asked to deliver this to Presley Barnett."

"Well, don't just stand there, give it to me." He held his hand out commandingly, snapping his fingers.

Once safely relieved of his delivery obligations, the stagehand bolted from the room without a backward glance.

"What did he want?" Mrs Barnett asked, striding into the room with Presley's discarded robe. Thankfully, the older woman didn't comment on finding him standing in her daughter's empty dressing room. From the open door, he could hear Presley talking to the crowd, them baying back their adoration.

"To give this to Presley." He held out the envelope.

"Well, bless your heart. Hand it over, then." No sooner had it settled in her palm when she flipped it over, brows furrowing when the other side showed no sign of writing. She swiftly slipped one of her nails into the corner to tear it open. Afterwards, Markus wasn't able to pinpoint what made him peer over her shoulder at the contents. Maybe it was the way her body tensed, the quiet intake of air, maybe even the way her mouth tightened. All he knew was that something in that envelope was very wrong.

A chill swept over him at the picture of Presley. She was sitting beside Kelly on a black leather sofa, each with a drink in their hand, deep in conversation. Scrawled across it in thick red marker was *Always watching you.* A cold rage unlike anything he'd felt before made his palms wet as he pulled his phone out and began to dial.

"Nate, I don't know where the heck you are, but if you're not here in thirty seconds, you're fired."

Mrs Barnett twisted her necklace around her finger, looking from him to the picture as if trying to make up her mind about something. Finally, she released the tormented jewelry from her grasp. "I think you should come with me."

It went against Markus's nature to go when summoned, but there was something to the way she said it that set his feet in motion after her. She led him to a little side room—one that could have easily been a janitor's closet—and took a key out of her pocket, unlocking it before swinging it wide and gesturing for him to go inside.

The air was stale, and it took a moment for Markus's mind to process what was inside. Stacks of mailbags fully filled half of the room and boxes—some with overflowing paperwork, others with a random assortment of things—took up half of the space that was left.

Nate chose that moment to appear. Markus waved him inside. "What is this?" His voice was shakier than he would have liked. Something about the room gave him the creeps.

"This is all the fan mail we get that falls in the undesirable category." She picked up some of the papers, fanning them out. "Letters that are obsessive, gifts that are inappropriate.

Don't even get me started on the emails and social media messages."

Markus felt like the air was being sucked out of the room, his stomach clenching as he wrapped his mind around what was in front of him. "Presley has stalkers." His voice was matter of fact.

"Every famous person has stalkers, and Presley is more famous than most people on the planet. It's part of being a performer, a celebrity. We keep files on everything and don't bother Presley with it." He couldn't understand why Mrs Barnett wasn't more riled at the danger her daughter faced every day.

He turned to Nate. "Did you know about this?"

The burly security boss looked up from the box he was rifling through. "No, boss."

Markus's fist balled. How had all of this been going on under his nose, in his casino? He took the picture of Presley that had been delivered that day and threw it at Nate. "How the heck did someone manage to take a picture of Presley? They even managed to get it delivered to her dressing room, for Pete's sake!" he demanded, the rage building up in him.

"We deemed the risk to her safety to be minimal while she was in the casino. At her and her mother's request, we don't have someone with her all the time." Nate faced him squarely, feet wide, like the soldier he had been.

"I don't care what she or her mother wants anymore. She isn't to go anywhere without one of your men with her. I want all of this stuff removed and placed in one of the spare conference rooms, and you're going to go through all of it." Markus glared at Mrs Barnett. "And since you don't seem to be taking this seriously, from now on, anything like this"—he gestured around the room—"comes straight to me for Nate to handle. Do I make myself clear?"

Mrs Barnett nodded, ashen faced. *Good. Maybe now she'll*

start protecting her daughter instead of acting like it's just part and parcel of being famous. Furiously clenching his jaw, he stalked from the room, Presley's words from the other night whispering in his mind. *I like to believe in the best in people.* He scowled. *Not in my casino.*

It was a grueling schedule for everyone involved with making each and every one of Presley's performances the success it was, from the lowliest runner to the sound production and her band. When she had the chance to throw a party, she liked to go big so they all knew just how much she appreciated them. Which is why, when she'd told Paul that she wanted to host a Halloween party, she'd told him she wanted no expense to be spared. As she looked around the conference hall they had commandeered for their party, it was obvious he'd hit the brief on the head.

"Do you like it?" Paul asked, dressed as a zombie jailbird and handing her a Bloody Mary. This time the drink really did live up to the name, filled with all manner of gruesome things. Presley couldn't be sure, but it looked like there might even be some sort of eyeballs floating around in the thick viscous liquid.

"It's spooktacular." Laughing, she pointed over to where her mother was dancing with Suzie, both dressed as wolves, her mama as the wolf dressed in grandma's clothing and

Suzie as a very naughty looking werewolf. "I'd say both of them are having a howling good time."

Paul smiled indulgently at her. "I see what you did there. And can I say, if I'd known that you and Mrs Barnett were going to dress as a theme, I would have offered myself as the Huntsman." He made a ferocious face as he took in her Little Red Riding Hood costume.

"I blame it on these drinks. I don't know what else is in the Halloween version of a Bloody Mary but, wow, they're good. I'm fixin' to have some more of them." She plucked a gummy spider from her glass and popped it in her mouth. "I'm sorry, I didn't even think to ask, but it would have been great if you'd been the Huntsman. The three of us would have looked awesome together."

"Like a matched set," he agreed.

Presley scanned the room. "Everyone looks like they're having a great time."

"How could they not? Great music, great food and drink, great company." For a moment, he studied her intently before an appealing smile appeared. "Would you like to dance with me?" Paul held his hand out.

"I'm sorry, but there's something I need to do first. Would you please excuse me?"

A shadow darkened his eyes, his smile freezing on his lips before his normal pleasant expression returned. "Of course. But I'm going to hold you to it when you come back."

"Gladly." She headed for the door. There was someone she needed to see. On her way past a waiter, she hooked a couple of shots off his tray that had been made to look like chicken fetuses. *Maybe I'd better have these first.*

～

THE ENERGY around the poker table shifted, becoming more primal and heated. Confused at the change, Markus sought to locate its cause, and then he saw her. Black high heels clicking on the polished floor, her short red cape flaring behind her as she glided into the room, all heads swinging her way. For a moment, all he could do was take in the vision that strode toward him, regal as a queen. To go with the rest of her ensemble, she wore black fishnet stockings, an embroidered peasant blouse and a short, flared skirt. Markus knew how the big bad wolf felt looking at Little Red Riding Hood.

Growling, he stood abruptly, the forgotten blonde who had been draped over him going flying and letting out a startled protest as she was laughingly caught by the man beside him. Every nerve in his body screamed at him to take his woman away from the hungry eyes gleaming at her. A dark swirl of jealousy mixed with fear that any one of them could be the one who sent the photograph. Heck, they could be any one of her numerous stalkers. He grabbed her by the arm and marched her from the room and to a quiet corner of an abandoned gaming area.

"If you wanted to hang out with me, then, suga, all you needed to do was come to my party." Markus stared at the rich chestnut curls that cascaded around her shoulders where her hood had fallen back. The light glinting off it looked like flames dancing. "Heck, I don't even care about the blonde you were wearing like a scarf." She drawled.

He blinked. *What blonde?* "I had other commitments."

Presley toyed with the roulette wheel on the table. "I could see." She pouted. "You'd have more fun at my Halloween party. We have the best drinks. They have eyeballs and everything."

"How many of these drinks have you had? And why are

you here by yourself?" When he caught up with Nate, he was going to give that man the chewing out of his life.

"Um, well, it depends. Are you talking big drinks or little drinks?"

"Just drinks in general."

"Three."

Markus peered at her. She was definitely tipsy for having only had three drinks. Not rotten drunk, but lacking her usual inhibitions. "I think I'd better call Nate and have him come down and get you."

"I have a better idea." She crooked her finger at him to lean closer, and for a moment, Markus's stomach quivered in anticipation of her inviting him upstairs. "If it lands on the red, you come back to the party with me."

He leaned back, momentarily rebuffed, then quickly regrouped his wits. "How about if it lands on black, you spend your next free day with me, doing whatever I say?"

"Deal accepted." She stuck her hand out for him to shake.

He accepted, her hand deliciously warm in his. "Would you care to do the honors?" He gestured at the wheel.

"It's the only way I know you won't cheat."

She plucked up a ball from where it lay motionless and set the wheel into motion, tossing it back in. Markus stopped breathing as it bounced and rocked around finally landing on … black. He allowed himself the pleasure of smiling smugly at her.

"I win."

"This time. How about best out of three?" Her eyes gleamed hopefully as she smiled winsomely at him from beneath lowered lashes.

"Nope. Every good gambler knows to leave the table when you're ahead." Markus brushed a curl back from her face. "And I'm ahead." Disappointed, he watched Nate appear. *About time. If I was someone who wanted to hurt her, I'd have done so by now.* "Ah, Nate, just in time to escort Presley back to her party."

"It's not true what they say anyway," Presley interrupted owlishly, her lush bottom lip sticking out.

He could only stare at her, baffled at the sudden change in subject. "What isn't true?"

"That blondes have more fun." *Back to the blonde again. Was she ... jealous?* The thought made his heart pound. She gave him a saucy little smile. "I can show you where the fun is. If you get bored with your other commitments—" Presley added air quotes for emphasis. *She must really be feeling her drinks to act like this.* "Come find me. I'll be hanging with all the cool kids at my Halloween party."

Markus wasn't even sure what, exactly, had just happened as he watched her skipping away, slightly unsteadily, beside the burly security man. But whatever it was, he felt like someone had turned the lights off and left him in the dark.

*P*resley was breathless as she stepped off the stage, her mother waiting with a robe and a bottle of lemon and honey water. "I think that was my best one yet."

"I thought you were fixin' to stay up there, you gave them so many encores. Those folks tonight won't be bellyaching that they didn't get their money's worth," Mama said as they headed to Presley's dressing room. Just before she opened the door for her daughter, Mrs Barnett surprised her by stopping, hand on the knob. She turned and took Presley's face between her hands and gently planted a kiss on her forehead. "Your father and I are very proud of you."

Presley blinked back tears at the sudden display of affection. Mama showed her love every single day by the million different things she did for her, but she wasn't often moved to physical demonstration. "Thanks, Mama. I love you and Daddy, too."

Mrs Barnett cleared her throat, turning back to open the door. Presley was still floating in the happy glow of her mother's love when she spotted the small floral arrangement on her dressing table. "Mama, you didn't need to get me flowers."

Her mother froze, her face going pale. "Let me take those." Mama quickly brushed past Presley, knocking her to one side in her haste to collect the flowers first.

Presley was more shocked than hurt. *Mama goes from loving to pushy in under a minute.* "Hang on, Mama. I want to have a look at them first." She reached out to retrieve them from her mother's uncommonly strong grip, a slight tousle ensuring. "Give them to me."

"Is everything all right in here?" Paul asked, making both women jump in surprise.

"Paul, would you be able to take these flowers for Presley?" Mrs Barnett quickly thrust them to the slightly bewildered man.

Presley, seeing her opportunity, quickly snatched them from his limp grasp. "Really, Mama, such a fuss." She looked down at the unusual arrangement made up of yellow carnations, orange lilies, purple petunias and black roses. Something seemed off about the choice of flowers the sender had selected, as though there was a deeper, more sinister motive. Presley shook the creepy feeling away. *You're being silly. They're just flowers, for Pete's sake.* "There doesn't appear to be a note." She looked up in time to catch the look that passed between Paul and her mama. Carefully, she set the flowers back down on the table. Hands on hips, she turned back, tapping her foot agitatedly. "What gives? Is one of y'all fixin' to tell me what's going on, or has the cat got your tongue?" She narrowed her eyes at Paul, figuring he was the one most likely to crack first.

Sure enough, he did. "Mrs Barnett, do you think we need to ramp up security?"

"Paul, why would we do that?" Presley pressed.

He swallowed, looking very much caught between a rock

and a hard place. "Um, well, it's just that we think those flowers might be from a stalker."

"Oh, piff." Mrs Barnett waved her hands in the air to dispel his comment as sheer nonsense. "An overzealous fan at best, child, and I'm sure the security we have is adequate. Especially now that Markus is personally overseeing it."

Presley blinked. She had a stalker—no, an overzealous fan—and Markus knew about it, and not only knew about it, but was concerned enough to be monitoring the situation himself? "I seem to be the only one who doesn't know what's going on here."

Mrs Barnett began to straighten up the room. Mama always needed to keep her hands busy when she didn't want to talk about something. "Let's just be vigilant and I'm sure there will be nothing to worry about."

Paul gave Presley a reassuring smile, seemingly grateful to take his lead from Mama. "And it's my job to make sure you're safe, and with Nate around, I'm sure you will be."

A powerful relief filled her. Of course there was nothing to worry about. She was making mountains out of molehills. "You do more than that, Paul. You're making my time here enjoyable. Are you fixin' to make it so I don't ever want to leave?" She couldn't resist teasing.

Red flowed up Paul's neck and onto his face and he seemed to find a spot down at his feet very interesting. "I'm glad you're happy here." He looked up at her, suddenly finding his confidence again. "What are your plans for your day off tomorrow? If you like, we could go and do some sightseeing." The words came out in a great rush.

"I'd love to"—his features brightened before she could finish—"except I already have plans with Markus tomorrow. Can I take a raincheck?"

"Of course." He quickly excused himself from the room. Presley felt bad that Paul was visibly crushed by the rejection, no matter how kindly given, and yet a thrill of anticipation went through her at what tomorrow would bring. *With Markus, anything could happen.*

PRESLEY'S liquid brown eyes opened wide, taking in the sight of him. "Are you actually wearing trainers?"

"Limited edition, but yes. Where we're going today, loafers weren't going to work." Avid curiosity danced across her features. "And no, I'm not going to tell you. Now, are you ready?"

"Yes." She gathered her bag and hesitantly closed the door behind her.

He had to give her credit, she didn't ask any more questions as they made their way down to his waiting car, nor when they settled in and pulled away from the casino. Her eyes did widen when it was apparent that their next stop was the airport, but still not a word until they were on the tarmac alongside his private plane.

"You do remember I have a show I need to perform tomorrow night, right?" she pointed out in bewilderment.

Markus stroked his chin. "Well, I'm sure they'll find someone to fill in for you if you're late."

"Markus!" she rounded on him. "That's not funny.

He watched her in smug delight, his new favorite pastime. "Well, I'll tell you this at least. I promise I'll have you back before the clock strikes midnight, Cinderella."

Somewhat pacified, she allowed the driver to help her from the car and followed him up the stairs to the plane. And still, she didn't ask anything more. At last, once the plane was in the air and the hostess was handing them champagne, she couldn't take it anymore.

"Do you always overcompensate this much?" Markus raised his eyes from the tablet he was watching.

"This is how I live."

"It might be how you live, but you try too hard to impress people, dominate them." She raised her glass to the sunlight streaming in, turning it to see the bubbles dancing in the pale gold liquid. "I'm not like them."

Markus quirked a brow at her. "Them?"

"Yes, them. The women who gather around you like moths to the flame, attracted by all the shiny wealth you project. I have plenty of my own money. I don't need you to flash yours around to impress me."

"Then what would impress you?" he drawled, stroking the beads of condensation on the side of his glass, striving to maintain a casual façade. At his core, every nerve was riveted, breathless in anticipation of what her response would be.

Those remarkable eyes of hers gazed at him from beneath her sooty lashes, considering him. "I would be impressed if I could see the real Markus."

Dread made the bright light of the cabin suddenly dull. *I'm doomed.* A horrible feeling of vulnerability made him want to hide. He didn't even know if he would recognize the real Markus, stripped of all his protective wealth and power. "Who says this isn't me?"

The way she looked at him, he felt like his soul was laid bare, exposed for her perusal. "You weren't always a casino owner. Before that, you were just a professional gambler."

"I was never just a professional gambler, I was *the* professional gambler." Markus couldn't believe it. She was acting like he was just one of many. He'd never been making up numbers or part of the crowd.

She smiled at him, eyes twinkling at his robust rebuttal. "My apologies, the professional gambler."

"Much better."

"But what were you before that?"

Markus shuddered inwardly, seeking an escape. The painful hand of memory took his heart firmly in its grasp, crushing it. "I lived with my mom." Presley looked like she wanted to ask more, but something in his gaze must have warned her that she'd received all she was going to get from him. "Your turn. What sort of name for a girl is Presley?"

"Only the best kind," she said indignantly. "My daddy was a studio drummer on Elvis's last album, so I was named after The King." Presley pursed her lips. "My full name is actually Presley Dolly Barnett."

Markus had to give her a close look to check if she was teasing him, but from her earnest expression, it appeared she was being truthful. "Your parents wanted you to be a singer then, even as a baby?"

"Mama used to sing to me when I was still in her belly. Daddy says that I even cried in perfect tune."

"Your parents aren't together anymore, are they?"

Presley's face scrunched up as she glared back at him. "What on earth makes you think that? Of course they're still together."

"It's just that your father isn't around, but your mom is."

"Daddy is working on an album back home in Nashville. He'll be finished in time for when we get back home for our Christmas break."

"Home's Nashville, then?" He knew she was from Tennessee but had never bothered to ask where she lived now—at least, when she didn't live at The Chimera.

"Our farm is just outside of it in a town called Franklin. It's just the prettiest place with a river. Daddy says that there might even be a chance that we'll get some snow there this year. I can't wait to go back. I'm counting the days."

Markus felt like she'd punched him in the gut. *She's*

counting the days until she can get away from me. "Sounds rustic, if you like that sort of thing," he said sourly.

Presley frowned at the tone in his voice but clearly chose not to pursue it. "I know I prattle on about going home for Christmas, but I just love that time of the year. Everyone coming together to put the tree up and have eggnog and hot cocoa. Don't even get me started on the carols."

"I'd love Christmas, too, if I was raking in royalties from a Christmas album like you."

She sighed. "I shouldn't have to explain to you that Christmas isn't about money. It's about the truly important things in life."

"That's what I just said."

She sighed again, disappointment seeping from every pore, and peered at him. "Do you spend Christmas at The Chimera?"

"Heck no."

She rolled her hands in the air, encouraging him to continue. When he wasn't forthcoming with more information, she rolled her eyes. It looked uncomfortably similar to Kelly's go-to expression. "So, what are you planning to do this year? Do you have a family tradition?"

"No." Cold, blunt, and he sure as heck didn't intend to elaborate on his family any more than that. "Last year, I went to St Moritz." He thought of the week filled with snow, parties, and brunettes, blondes and redheads. "Maybe this year I'll go to an island I'm considering buying. Or I do have my mega yacht. I could sail around the Greek Islands."

"It doesn't sound very Christmassy if you ask me. Give me the farm with my family and Walter anytime."

Jealousy speared him. "Who's Walter?"

"He lives at the farm. He's been a part of my life for three years now." She smiled sweetly as though just thinking about him made her happy. As the plane flew onward to their destination, Markus began to have some dark thoughts about what he would like to do to this mysterious Walter.

"I can't believe you did this for me." The way she looked at him made his stomach do belly flops. When her hand quietly slipped into his, he had such an intense feeling of protectiveness sweep over him. She was a strong independent woman, and yet, standing there watching the private fireworks he'd organized—well, his PA had organized—he was suddenly conscious of how little she was. He could feel the delicate bones of her hand. Like a bird.

"So, I impressed you a little, then?" Markus couldn't resist looking smugly down at her.

"Yeah, you did. I've never had an entire theme park just to myself." The fireworks were reflected in her eyes as she looked up at him, joyous as a kid on the fourth of July. "Thank you. I think I needed this break from all the pressures of my show, you know?" Markus knew in that moment that he'd do anything to get her to look at him like that again. There was no escaping she was his new addiction.

"Anyone else and I would have whisked them off for dinner overlooking the Eiffel Tower. But somehow I knew taking you on a rollercoaster was going to get me the most brownie points."

"I didn't know you were even worried about brownie points." She gave him a teasingly challenging look but made no attempt to remove her hand from his.

"I worry about a lot of things with you. I've never done that with anyone else." He had to fight an overwhelming need to be closer to her. Suddenly holding her hand wasn't enough. Such an attraction could be perilous.

With a deliberate casualness, he released his hold and

moved to stand in front of her. He reached out, his knuckles grazing softly against her cheek, a tremor going through her when they touched. Presley stared back at him, her gaze as soft as a caress. He couldn't fight the pull he felt toward her anymore. Putting a large hand on her waist, he drew her close to him. She wound her arms inside his jacket and around his back. Slowly, in exquisite torment, he lowered his head.

"This is me." His lips brushed hers as he spoke, and then he lost himself in the lingering kiss, savoring every moment. But in that kiss, he was also found.

Presley couldn't help it. Her sense of humor took over and she burst out laughing as Suzie danced around with a prop candy cane. Only moments earlier, she'd pushed Presley out of the way to show her how the experts did it. Paul cleared his throat.

"Sorry to be the party pooper in the room, but Presley, I need you to focus."

She straightened in her chair. "Yes, Paul." She smiled winsomely up at him. Paul went a bright scarlet. *He really is such a sweetheart.*

"As I was saying, the props are ready." He cast a reproachful glare to where Suzie was still capering about like a psychedelic Christmas elf. "Mrs Barnett, I believe the costumes are under control?" He quirked a questioning brow at her mother.

"Yes, Paul. Final fittings are in the next few days, but I don't anticipate any problems." Mrs Barnett looked up from her magazine. "Suzie, child, unless you're fixin' on a career that doesn't involve working with Presley, I suggest you put it away now."

"Yes, Mrs Barnett." Suzie quickly set the oversized Christmas ornament in the corner and perched on the dressing table.

Mrs Barnett returned her attention to her daughter. "Presley, have you finished your song list yet?"

"Yes. I thought I emailed it through to you?" Presley pursed her lips and pulled out her phone to double check. "Nope, it's sitting in drafts. I'll send it now."

"I swear, child, you've been slower than molasses since your date with Markus." Mama's words were softened by her teasing wink, but still Presley felt her cheeks warm at her comment.

"I'd be in shock, too, after the trauma of going on a date with Markus," Suzie said in solidarity with Presley. She leaned forward, chin in her hands. "Was it awful?"

How to describe the monumental shift in her perception of Markus? Darn, but he was a complicated man with an exterior fashioned to make himself unlikable and in control. Presley was more convinced than ever that it was a façade he'd created long ago to protect himself. She wondered what had been so catastrophic that he'd chosen to become the megalomaniac he was now over who he had been.

"Well he hired out an entire theme park just for us."

"What!?!" squealed Suzie. "So, you didn't have to wait in line for any of the rides?"

Presley laughed at her friend's enthusiasm. "Nope. And then, when it got dark, there was a fireworks display." She didn't think everyone needed to know about the kiss that followed. *A gal was allowed a few secrets.*

Suzie sighed dreamily. "If a man did that for me, I'd marry him."

Paul's frown turned disapproving. In fact, it was the first time Presley had ever seen an expression on the manager's face other than a variation of pleasant. "I think you'll find she has better taste in men than that." *Oops, did she?*

The makeup artist wasn't about to let a little censor stop her. She held her knuckle to her mouth, barely suppressing her excitement. "Does this mean you're going to go on another date with him?"

Would she? Oh, who was she kidding? If he asked, she'd say yes. "He hasn't asked me out on another one," she stalled.

"Well, I think that man is all sorts of hard work," Mama said.

"Speaking of work, I've had a request from the couple who won the charity prize a while back," Paul said. "You remember your biggest fans?"

"How could I forget?" There was a trace of laughter in her voice.

"Well, they've made contact and, as mentioned, since they are your biggest fans, they want tickets to your Christmas show." He peered at her questioningly. "What do you want me to tell them?"

"What are ticket sales like?" Mrs Barnett asked him.

"Sold out."

"But there are always spare tickets floating about," Presley said.

"True, but the question is do you want them to have tickets? They were"—Paul gathered his thoughts—"a bit full on last time."

"Oh my gosh, weren't they?" Suzie giggled. "They were next level."

"See if you can find some, but don't put too much effort into it. If you can't find anything, explain it to them." Presley was relieved when her mother made the decision for her.

"They won't be happy," Presley said, remembering how zealous they'd been in their adoration.

"Bless them, they'll get over it." Mama didn't seem like she was going to lose any sleep over the outcome. "Now, child, time for you to grab a light supper before it's time to finish off your hair and makeup."

Her stomach rumbled. She hadn't even known she was hungry before her mother spoke. *Funny how Mama always knew best.*

~

THE SCREAM CUT through Markus like a knife. Frantically, he bolted the last few feet to Presley's dressing room, all thought of asking permission to play her Christmas carols in the casino fleeing before an onslaught of pure adrenaline to protect his woman.

When some semblance of normal thought returned, he had the sobbing Presley in his arms. He quickly took in the chair that was toppled over, obviously in her haste to get away from the dressing table.

"Presley, baby girl, what happened?" A cold knot formed in his stomach as her slight body trembled.

She pointed an unsteady finger toward the table. Mystified, he peered, leaning closer. One of her promotional flyers for her Christmas performance lay discarded on the table, her eyes stabbed out and a target drawn over her face. Markus felt as though a hand had tightened around his throat.

"Presley, where is everyone? Why are you here alone?" He knew fear made his voice rough. The thought of someone getting this close to Presley in his casino made violent impulses course through him.

Presley gave a little sniffle. "Mama went to get me something to eat. I went to the bathroom and, when I came back, that was there." She shivered, and Markus tightened his arms reassuringly around her. "I hate feeling scared like this," she said in a small voice.

"And you shouldn't have to. Nate's about to lose his job." Markus wanted to throttle the security manager over his failure. He quickly freed an arm and dialed Nate's number, curtly telling him of the predicament before hanging up on him.

"What on God's green earth is going on?" Mrs Barnett glared at Presley in Markus's arms.

"I thought you said Presley had nothing to worry about— it was just part of the business," Markus hurled at the older woman, gesturing at the dressing table in disgust. It was with some small measure of satisfaction that he saw her face go chalky as she picked up the flyer with shaky hands.

"Presley, child, I'm so sorry, but everything's going to be all right." A sense of profound loss sapped Markus of strength when Presley left his embrace to go to her mother's open arms. *Didn't she know that he could keep her safe?*

"Markus, I don't know how this happened." Nate strode into the room with several of his men. *Wise to bring body-guards, but they won't save you.*

"I pay you to know. Check all footage, I want answers. And from now on, Presley is never left alone. And by that, I don't mean in her mother's company or Paul's or that kaleidoscope fairy. She has proper security around the clock." When Markus got his hands on whoever was doing this, he was going to enjoy making them pay. *No one threatened his woman and got away with it.*

~

"CHILD, if you want to cancel, ain't no one going to blame you." Mama kept looking around like she expected the boogie man to jump out at any moment. It rattled Presley to see her mother so spooked.

Presley drew in a deep breath and forbade herself from trembling. "But I'd blame myself. I can't let my fans down for one looney."

Her mother pressed her lips tightly together. "I'm sure Paul could make everything all right by the fans, offer them new tickets. Markus might even throw in a bonus to sweeten it." Mrs Barnett looked to Paul for support.

"Of course." He nodded in agreement. "We need to do what's best for you, Presley."

Presley tossed her chestnut hair over her shoulder in a gesture of defiance. "What's best for me is for Suzie to touch up my makeup. I'm going on stage one way or another. So, you can either help me get ready or get out of the way."

Suzie began to fuss around, brushing at Presley's face. Paul looked at Mrs Barnett doubtfully. "I think we should at least wait until Nate's men have time to do another sweep of the stage and seating. Maybe even till he has a chance to view the tapes." He trailed off, waiting for guidance from the older woman.

Cold fear made Presley's palms sweat. *I will not allow anyone to stop me from doing what God put me on this earth to do.* Determinedly, she balled her hand into a fist as if she could take her terror and harness it somehow. "No, nothing is going to happen to me up there. Now, get them to raise the curtain. I'm going on." Before anyone could say another word, she strode out. There was a great whoosh, and then the crowd, her fans, her people, roared their love for her.

There, in the golden spotlight, nothing could touch her. She was invincible.

Markus stared at his steepled fingers, the silence stretching. "Let me make sure I understand you correctly"—his voice was cold and lashing—"that somehow there was a camera malfunction that only happened in Presley's dressing room and only for twenty minutes. Not to mention in a security system that cost several million dollars and now we have no footage of who put that flyer in Presley's room." *How can I protect her against something I don't know?* His anger became a scolding fury. "Tell me how that happened." He smashed his fist down onto the desk, sending pain shooting up his arm. Nate, for his part, stood ramrod straight at attention in front of him, taking the umbrage with a neutral expression.

"That's the state of affairs as it stands. I have my best technicians working on the system to see if there is any possible way of retrieving the footage or if the glitch is irreversible." Nate maintained steady, even eye contact, not showing the least hint of intimidation.

"Tell him he can't do that." Presley barged in, Paul trailing behind her, awkwardly looking at Markus in apology, Mrs Barnett bringing up the rear.

"Sure, come right on in, Presley. It's not like the door was shut for a reason," Markus sneered sarcastically. He knew his tone would hurt her, but it was better than letting her run roughshod over him. She might not like what he was doing, but at least she would be safe.

Presley planted her hands on her hips, fire blazing from her eyes. "Tell Paul that he can't cancel my shows."

"Now, why would I do that when I'm the one who told him to do it?" he drawled with distinct mockery.

"Well, you can't." Her glare burned through him.

"Try me, baby girl." Markus returned her fire with pure ice.

Triumphantly, she held a bound document aloft. "Well, suga, this says you can't."

"Is that a contract? Mrs Barnett, is she actually waving her contract around at me? I don't care what it says. Until future notice, all your performances have been canceled." He insisted with growing impatience.

"Suga, I'm right torn up about what happened, too, but Presley's right." Mrs Barnett walked forward, placing her hand on Presley's shoulder in support. "It's her decision if she wants to cancel the shows or not, and that contract backs it up."

Markus ground his teeth in frustration. Heaven save him from beautiful, smart, determined country singers. *Why can't she just do what she's told?* "Then I want the Christmas show canceled. That flyer could be some sort of warning about it."

"No way." Presley boldly met his eyes. "I won't let my fans down."

"You don't think getting killed by a random crazy won't let them down?" Markus sneered, frustration that she was willing to put herself in danger making bile burn the back of his throat.

"You won't let that happen." With a saucy toss of her chestnut hair, Presley strutted out of the room to leave Paul helplessly shrugging at his fuming boss. *Mrs Barnett should have given that girl more spankings when she was growing up.*

~

PRESLEY KICKED an unoffending cushion out of her way. *That arrogant, condescending male chauvinist jerk! Telling me what I can and can't do.* "Who does he think he is?" She swung for the cushion a second time, misjudged, and her big toe connected with the floor. Dropping like a sack of potatoes, she hit the floor, clutching at her foot. *Now look what he's done.*

Mrs Barnett walked in, carrying costumes over her arms, Suzie and Paul similarly loaded, took in her groaning daughter with raised eyebrows, and simply stepped over her to get past. Paul helped Presley to her feet. "He's only doing what he thinks is best."

"Don't you stand up for him," Presley cried. "I thought you were on my side."

"I am," Paul quickly hastened to assure her. "But I also work for him. I think this time he's right."

"Child, leave the poor man alone," her mother interjected.

Presley pushed her hair back from her face. "Which one?"

"Paul. I guess you should probably leave Markus alone, too, but I'm actually fond of Paul." Her mother glanced at her watch. "When you're finished bellyaching, go change into the Mrs Claus outfit. Suzie will help you, and then get your hair and makeup done."

Presley muttered mutinously under her breath as Suzie assisted her in getting dressed. Outside of the change room, she could hear her mother chattering away to Paul.

"Your mom's really taken to him, hey?" Suzie whispered. "Considering it hasn't been that long. She took a whole year to be nice to me."

"It wasn't that she was horrible," Presley said, defending her mother. "She just takes a while to warm up to people. Well, normally. She's been burned a few times, and that's kinda made her gun-shy now."

"I can imagine." Suzie sponged concealer onto Presley's face. "Thank you for the invitation for Thanksgiving dinner. Mrs Barnett said your daddy was coming, too."

A wide grin split Presley's face and she bounced a little on her chair. "Yep. He finished up the album a bit earlier than expected, so he's going to fly out here for a couple of days and then home to the farm. I've made him promise to not go Christmas tree shopping till I get there."

Suzie laughed. "You and Christmas. But won't all the good trees be gone by the time you get back home?"

"But the tree I'm meant to have will still be there."

Presley could almost smell the fir needles as she pictured the perfect tree in her mind. An image of dark hair and pale blue eyes replaced her daydream of greenery. She didn't care what Markus had said. She felt sad thinking about how he was planning on spending his Christmas. His version of the holiday was empty, soulless, and he hadn't even mentioned what he was doing for Thanksgiving. A secretive smile crept along her lips. Maybe she could corrupt him into the proper meaning of the festive season one holiday at a time.

There were definitely perks to having a props department. Presley surveyed the suite in satisfaction, taking in the harvest theme of pumpkins, squash, cornucopias, and miniature scarecrows that served as the table centerpiece. There were even piles of autumn leaves that had been placed in the corner of the room with more pumpkins and larger versions of the table decorations. It was in stark contrast to the over-the-top glitzy Christmas decorations that were festooned about the casino. Heck, they'd even started playing her Christmas carols over the speakers.

This year Mama had begged off doing the cooking honors, explaining it was just too hard to do it without the kitchen equipment she was familiar with. After much promising that next year, in the sanctuary of the farm, she would lay out all the trimmings, they'd agreed to order it from The Chimera kitchens. *It wasn't like they'd exactly been left to slum it.*

Presley paced the room for the umpteenth time. Mama was collecting Daddy from the airport, and the sudden sense of being alone made the apartment feel empty. She briefly considered inviting the security guy who had been posted outside her room in for company but decided against it when she thought of how much trouble he would be in with Markus if he accepted. *Ah, Markus. My complicated little onion.* She'd been astounded when he'd accepted her invitation to Thanksgiving dinner, even after she'd made it abundantly clear that it wasn't going to be just the two of them and that the other attendees included some of his employees and both of her parents.

Presley began to ponder what, exactly, she wanted from him. There was no denying the attraction that sparked between them whenever they were in the same room, but was that all it was? And what would happen at the end of her residency? She would go back to the farm, record more albums, go on more tours. But Markus, would he want to stay here at The Chimera where he was in control?

The sound of a door closing echoed in the back of Presley's head, making her jump in alarm. Cool relief hit her hard when the object of her thoughts strode into the room. *Trust Markus not to bother with knocking.* His gaze traveled over her face and searched her eyes—for what, Presley could not be sure. Something intense passed between them, unspoken, setting a tingling in the pit of her stomach.

"Did everyone hear I was coming and begged off?" Markus's mouth twisted into a self-deprecating sneer.

Presley handed him a bottle of champagne to open. *Might as well put the man to work.* "Hardly. You are, in fact, early. Mama and Daddy will be here any minute, and the others will hopefully be on time."

No sooner had the cork popped and the champagne that fizzed out was expertly caught in a glass by Markus when, true to her words, her parents arrived. Excitedly, she hugged her father. Having missed him greatly while they were parted, her feelings were somewhat tempered by the disappointment of having her time with Markus interrupted. From there, her guests arrived in quick succession, exclaiming over the Thanksgiving décor and helping themselves to the champagne that Markus graciously continued to pour for them. Presley couldn't resist cocking a brow at him in question at his ongoing servitude.

"I'd call some staff up here to do this, but it appears the room is full of my employees whom I'm waiting on," he grumbled at her.

"Then it will make a nice change for everyone." Presley rested her hand on his arm lightly.

"And who is this young man?" her father asked, having settled his things into Mama's room and was now mingling with the guests.

Presley resisted the urge to jerk her hand back. Pridefully, she lifted her chin. Let everyone see, including her parents. "Daddy, this is Markus Jamison, he's the owner of The Chimera. Markus, this is my daddy, Mr Barnett."

Both men stood stiffly, appraising the other. Presley's head swiveled between the two, breath held, unsure how this meeting would go. Markus extended his hand first. "I'm glad you're here. It's been the bane of my life keeping your daughter out of trouble this past while."

Daddy grasped Markus's hand firmly. "It's been the bane of my life for years. I was glad when I heard there was someone to help me now." Her father's gaze was direct. Markus, unflinching, nodded.

"Oh, my. You should have seen the lines for the buffet," Suzie said, new beau in tow. The moment between the two men in her life—*was Markus serious enough to be a man in her life?*—was shattered.

"I quite like a buffet," Nate said, standing beside his tiny, dark-haired wife. It was quite a contrast between the grizzled, burly security man and the exotic beauty.

"Of course you do." Paul laughed, the only person who hadn't brought a plus one.

"Buffets are just a cesspool of germs. If you eat at them, you're just fixin' to get sick," Mama interjected. "Fancy going to a buffet for Thanksgiving. It's meant to be spent with family."

Presley looked around at the people she cared about in the room, her gaze lingering on the enigmatic dark-haired casino owner. *Yep, just like I'm doing.*

THE ROOM WAS full of happy chatter. People sat relaxed over empty plates, their bellies full and content. All around him, Markus had caught snippets of conversation, little insights into the people who worked for him. People he'd been more than happy to know only in passing and then only to better use their capabilities for his own purposes.

He didn't know that Nate was a passionate breeder of Alaskan Malamute dogs with his wife and that, when he retired, he wanted to move to Alaska and train full-time in dog sledding. Rainbow Brite had been the makeup artist on some of his favorite films and the stories she'd regaled the table with had been extraordinary. Paul had seemed content to listen. A few times, Markus had caught the PR manager staring at him where he sat between Presley and her father.

Now, he was an interesting old man. Markus had money and power. He could snap his fingers and get whatever his heart desired. He glanced at Presley. *Well, most of the time.* But the old man had reeked of coolness. He'd come through playing with the greats in dives and bars when music was all you needed. Markus couldn't help but admire him. Sure, the dinner hadn't turned out as ghastly as he'd anticipated, but he hoped to not be forced to rub shoulders with his employees in his leisure time anytime soon.

Finally, after lingering long into the evening, the sated guests made their way home, Markus with them. Why, then, did it feel that, as he headed to his own suite, he was leaving it instead?

A giant Christmas tree, oversized star jauntily on top, almost knocked Presley to the ground as it went by, and she was genuinely fearful for the continued safety of the golden ornament atop it. Around her, backstage props were being moved into place while dancers in various costumes of elves, sugar plum fairies and angels stretched. She couldn't help herself. There was something about a Christmas concert in Las Vegas that had made her want sparkles and cheesy costumes and yes, if she was honest, over the top. Not that tonight she felt much Christmas spirit in her soul.

She smiled at Bruno, the latest of Nate's men who had been assigned to follow her around. He gave a slight twitch of his lips before catching himself and returning to his habitual stern expression. *Way to suck all the holiday spirit out of the room.* Looking at him, she couldn't hide from the undeniable and dreadful fact that somewhere, maybe just around the corner, someone could be watching her. A cold sweat broke out over her forehead and she began to shake as fearful images built in her mind.

"Now I know why Santa Claus only wants to be away

from Mrs Claus for a night." Markus smiled wide in approval of her outfit. "I must say, red is your color." He reached out and brushed back a stray tendril from her face, his fingers lingering.

"Well, Mrs Claus isn't followed around all the time and snooped on," she snapped. Presley knew it was petty, but she needed someone to lash out on, to unleash the fear and uncertainty that buffeted her. Markus, with his smug, perfect face and complete control, was a safe target. That wasn't to say she was proud of herself for feeling that way.

The polished veneer hardened on his face. "I won't apologize for trying to keep you safe."

"I don't need you to keep me safe. I've been just fine for years." Presley heard the bitterness spill over into her voice. The silence lengthened between them, making her feel uncomfortably aware of how much of a brat she sounded like.

A muscle jerked angrily in Markus's jaw. He grasped her upper arms, the pressure verging on painful. Markus lowered his face until it was inches from hers. Presley wanted to protest, but she was silenced by his dark, angry glare. "From what I've seen in the boxes your mama kept hidden from you, it was just dumb luck nothing bad has happened sooner. You're the one who wanted the shows to continue. But remember, my casino, my rules."

Markus stood there, boldly intimidating for a moment longer, before roughly releasing Presley. She staggered back, off kilter. A look of implacable determination swept over his face and, with a final glare, he spun and was gone.

"You don't scare me you know!" she called to his departing back. *It's not you I'm scared of.*

~

Fake snow mixed with glitter sparkled and shimmered as it drifted down from the ceiling, coating the performers and turning the stage into a magical winter wonderland. Presley had the crowd eating out of her hand with her jokes and anecdotes of Christmases past in the Barnett household.

Markus was still grinding his teeth at her reckless stubbornness. He'd had to walk away before he'd started yelling to try to get some sense into that pretty little head of hers. *How can she be so blind to the danger she's in?* Every night, he went over camera footage, following her movements throughout the day, checking for anything that seemed out of the ordinary. Long after he'd gone to bed, he'd torment himself with what could happen to her, and then suffocating fear would make him gasp for breath.

"Ladies and gentlemen, I want y'all to put your hands together to welcome my mama to the stage." Mrs Barnett strode out into the spotlight wearing a green version of her daughter's outfit. Markus had to give it to them. The two women on stage, both spitting images of each other, were an arresting sight. It gave him pause to think that Presley would still be a beautiful woman even at that age. Visions of what a lifetime with her would be like tormented him. Heck, given how they'd just fought, maybe they wouldn't live that long.

On stage, Presley and her mother perched on stools in front of several enormous snowmen. The music had started, and both women were swaying to the music. Then Mrs Barnett opened her mouth and a voice as rich and smooth as caramel flowed out. It was a shock to appreciate her as a famous artist in her own right, having only viewed her as Presley's mother and manager. But tonight she shone in her own right.

Suddenly, Presley lifted her mic, and together their vocals wrapped around and blended, the harmony flawless. A shiver ran up his spine, an intense feeling of foreboding leaving his palms sweating. *Something's not right.* Paralyzed, he watched as, like in a movie, one of the snowmen began to slowly topple forward. Cries of alarm rang out from the crowd. Confused, Presley began to look around, her and Mrs Barnett never once breaking their song. And then they disappeared, swallowed by the enormous white stage prop.

Afterwards, Markus wouldn't be able to explain how he got backstage, pushing against the panicked crowd, the disgust as some stopped to hold phones aloft to capture the moment, the need to inflict pain on them. The thunderous beating of his heart as his legs turned into iron springs, propelling him forward as security swarmed the stage, the curtain dropping at last.

And then suddenly he was there, the deadly snowman already removed from the prone bodies. Mrs Barnett was groaning, clutching at her arm. *If she's making noise, she's okay.* It was Presley, chalky pale, her lips having an unnatural blue tinge to them as she lay deathly quiet and unmoving who made icy fear slide down his spine. *No, no, no. This can't be happening.*

Someone had called the paramedics and they pushed him out of the way. Paul stood beside Markus, his mouth moving, wringing his hands, but Markus couldn't hear a sound. It was like someone had pressed a mute button on the scene. Nate, face like a thunder cloud, was aggressively gesturing at his men—*a bit late now*—no doubt securing the area. And still, Presley didn't move. Not when they put her on a stretcher. Not when they carried her away. Not when he clasped her hand on the long ride to the hospital.

A fear so black it threatened to swallow him whole took hold, consuming him. *I've only just found you, Presley. Don't leave me now.* And then he did something he hadn't done for years.

He prayed.

CHAPTER 14

"You've had a concussion and some bruising, but I'd say you're one very lucky lady to escape with only that. All you need is to rest for a few days, and you'll be good as new." The doctor kept giving her little sideways glances, and Presley knew what was coming before he even opened his mouth. "I'm a huge fan, Miss Barnett. Can I get a photo with you?"

She nodded, the slight movement sending a spasm of pain rocketing through her skull. With grim determination, she pushed it away, focusing on smiling at the camera that a nurse who had been pressed into photographer duty now held.

"What do you think you're doing?" Markus bellowed, knocking the nurse out of his way as he grabbed the doctor and sent him flying. His handsome features were contorted with rage.

"She said it was okay," protested the doctor, backing up hastily.

"You're her doctor and she's just had a head injury. On what planet do you think it's okay to ask her to pose for a selfie?" His brows were dark slashes on his face.

Shame faced, the doctor quickly mumbled an apology before beating a quick retreat from the room. "Markus, it's no good getting your britches all in a bunch, or are you fixin' to act like a Neanderthal every time a fan interacts with me?" It might have been the head knock, but there had been something hot about Markus in aggressive protector mode. *Probably just the concussion.*

"Your mother is in the other room getting her arm looked at. It appears that it's a clean break, so shouldn't cause too much drama for her healing. And I've been told you need to spend the night in here for observation." Markus hesitated, measuring her for a moment. "Do you know how close you came tonight to that being very bad? As in, dead bad?" His crystal blue eyes drilled into her, giving her no inch to wiggle away. "From now on, we're doing things my way."

"I know." Presley's voice sounded as hollow as she felt. She was so darn tired of feeling scared. She was shocked when his eyes filled with a fierce sparkling.

"I will not tolerate anything happening to you. Have I made myself clear?"

"Is this your way of saying you care?" Presley said, again surprised by this unpredictable man.

"I care enough that I've stationed some bodyguards outside this room," he said, brushing her question off. *So much for having a moment.*

"I'm in a hospital. Don't you think you're being a bit ridiculous?"

Those eyes of his lashed her dangerously. Markus was clearly not in a trifling mood. "No, I don't. The first thing I learned in life was that anything precious needs to be protected. That's what I'm doing." There it was again, a hint at deeper emotions, but grudgingly extracted as though the admission was painful for him. "It's why safes were invented. To keep dirty poor people away from their betters' possessions."

Presley gave a horrified gasp, actually astonished that he could utter such derogatory nonsense. "I beg your pardon. You did not just say what I think you said."

He always did this—sucked her in until she thought she saw something genuine underneath and then spat her out with how much of a jerk he was. And yet, for that moment, she'd felt protected and precious in his eyes, and she didn't know whether she liked it or hated herself for feeling that way. She sighed, weary of the argument. *It's the concussion. I'm sure it's just that.*

GUT-WRENCHING sickness still swirled in his stomach, making him clench his teeth every time he thought about what had happened up on that stage. He'd never liked Christmas before. Now he positively detested it. *That, and darn snowmen!*

"Um, excuse me, visiting time is over. I have to ask you to leave." The nurse's voice was softly hesitant. Most of her body remained in the safety of the corridor as if to facilitate a quick escape if required.

"I don't think so." Markus returned to idly flicking through the stock exchange app on his phone.

The little nurse cleared her throat. This time, when she spoke, her voice was more forceful. "It's hospital policy, and I'm afraid I have to insist."

"Who's the boss of this hospital?"

"Mr Connors. Why?" It was satisfying to see the uncertainty flicker across her face. That was something he knew how to use.

"Leave her alone, Markus." Presley sighed from the bed, her voice weary.

"I was just—" She held up a hand, halting his protest.

"I don't care. She's just doing her job, and you're being a bully. Go home." Presley's words brooked no argument, even if Markus's heart clenched at the idea of leaving her here. *How can I protect her if I'm not here? Darn it!*

"Fine." Markus stalked out, not giving Presley another glance, knowing that his resolve would weaken if he saw her lying, pale, in bed. He did amuse himself by not altering his course and causing the nurse to bump her shoulder on the doorframe as she rapidly backed up to allow him to exit. She went chalky white, her eyes wide as he leaned his face in close to hers.

"If anything happens to her while I'm gone, I will hold you personally responsible, and you won't enjoy what happens after that." She swallowed as she nodded rapidly like a bobble head.

Not content, Markus speared the bodyguards he'd stationed outside Presley's room with a coldly threatening glare. "If either of you know what is in your best interest, you'll heed what I just said to her." Their nods were slightly more stoic, if no less quick to respond. Knowing there was nothing more he could do here, he resolved to have answers by morning.

Paul and Nate were waiting for him in his office, awkwardly sitting like schoolboys sitting in the principal's office when he entered.

"What do you want me to tell the press?" Paul twisted his phone around in his hand.

Fury almost choked Markus. "Don't you mean to ask how Presley or her mother are doing?"

Paul swallowed, his Adam's apple bobbing. "I—I—of

course. I just assumed that, if it was serious, you would have called. How are they?"

Markus fixed him with an icy glare, enjoying watching the PR manager squirm like a fish on a hook. "As you said, they're fine."

"I'm glad they're only a little banged up," Nate said, his steady, gravelly voice at odds with Paul's nervousness. "It could have been worse."

Now it was Nate's turn to be on the end of Markus's frosty gaze. "And it was your job to make sure something like that didn't happen."

"But what do I tell the press?" interrupted Paul. *Kelly wouldn't be here wasting my time with idiotic questions!*

"Spin it. Tell them Presley's fine. That this was always going to be her last show of the year. That she's going to have some much-needed family time over the holiday season and be back bigger and better than ever. I don't care. Think of something for yourself. It's why I pay you." A dark expression, shocking in its intensity, shadowed Paul's face before he scuttled from the room.

"Have you found out how it happened?" Markus asked Nate.

Nate's face twisted into a frustrated grimace. "No. No one was near the props who wasn't supposed to be. Everyone swears it was put in the correct spot and shouldn't have toppled." He shrugged. "Maybe it was an accident."

"I don't have accidents at The Chimera and sure as heck not ones that leave my star performer and her mother in hospital. You better find out exactly what when wrong."

"Yes, boss."

Alone, Markus poured himself a scotch from the crystal decanter. His hand trembled with barely contained fury, his ears pounding with an overpowering need for revenge. *Someone is going to pay for this.*

~

MARKUS TOYED with a deck of cards, flipping them between his fingers. Upstairs in her suite, Presley was no doubt preparing to head home the next day. A soft knock made his head jerk up. The lights gleamed on the waves in Presley's chestnut hair, putting him in mind of a moth drawn to the flame.

"I just wanted to thank you for the use of your plane tomorrow."

Markus wondered if she was aware of just how captivating a picture she made when she smiled. *Probably.* He looked back down. Anything to break the spell. "I didn't have any plans for it." The cards flicked faster and faster.

Undeterred, she took the seat across from his desk. "Have you decided what you're fixin' to do for Christmas? Did you end up buying that island?"

"Yeah, I did. I might go there. I'm not sure yet."

"How about I give you another option?" She gave him a saucy smile. "You know, you're like sour candy. You sure do make my mouth pucker, but darn it, if I'm not starting to get a taste for it." Markus blinked, baffled as to whether he had just been insulted or complimented. "So, here's what I'm proposing." Presley reached across the table and took the cards from his hands. "Are you willing to gamble on spending Christmas with me? Whoever pulls out the highest card wins. If I win, you come and spend it with me and my family on the farm doing Christmas my way. If you win, you can spend it however you like."

There was a challenge in her eyes that Markus found irresistible. He gestured to Presley to take a card. She gave a delighted grin when she pulled out the ten of spades. Markus reached across for the deck, his hand hesitating over the cards. Slowly, he extracted one and turned it over. Six of diamonds.

"Looks like I'm doing Christmas your way."

Presley clapped her hands excitedly. "Do you mean it? Are you actually going to go ahead with it?"

Seeing her so happy at the idea of spending Christmas with him did funny things to his soul. "A deal's a deal."

"You won't regret it." She stood excitedly. "I have to go tell Mama and, of course, let Daddy know to make up one of the guest rooms. Remember to pack warm." And then she fairly skipped from the room.

Presley didn't need or want anything from him. The realization soothed him in ways he'd never felt before. Still, it terrified him that he couldn't use it to control her. She was famous enough and wealthy enough to get everything she ever wanted or needed for herself. And yet, she'd asked him to join her on a holiday with her family that was obviously special to them. He mulled it over as he pulled out the card he'd slipped up his sleeve earlier—the first card he'd selected. There had never been a doubt in his mind that he wasn't going to play the card. Standing, he tossed it onto the desk. It fluttered through the air until it landed.

The queen of hearts.

MARKUS WAITED beside the sleek gleaming limo, giving last minute instructions to Lachlan for while he was gone. Irritation made him glance at his watch when he saw Paul making a beeline for him. "I think that's everything, Lachlan."

"I caught you before you left." Paul was obviously immune to Markus's glares, or maybe his sunglasses dulled their potency. "I've started spinning the story on what happened, but as it gets better traction, I'll be in touch. Which hotel will you be staying at in Nashville?"

Markus glanced again at his watch. *What was taking them so long?* "I'm not."

"Oh, you're not staying in Nashville? I thought that's why you were sharing a flight with Mrs Barnett and Presley?"

"I'm spending Christmas with them at their farm." Paul's mouth snapped shut in surprise. Relief that he could leave the annoying PR manager behind for a couple of weeks suddenly made the idea of the trip so much sweeter. "Ah, the ladies have arrived." Markus held the door to the limo open for them. "Now, if you'll excuse me, Paul. We don't want to be late, after all." Markus couldn't resist a little wave as the limo door slammed shut in the other man's face.

"It's very nice of you to let us use your plane," Mrs Barnett said, pulling her coat more comfortably around her body.

"Well, I certainly wasn't going to fly commercial," he said, horrified at the thought.

"And there's the gracious Markus we all know and love." Presley laughed. And just like that, the world stopped for him. Somehow, hearing her say his name and love in the same sentence, the carefree laugh, or even the way her and her mother were now discussing what Christmas presents they'd bought and what they still needed to go shopping for did funny things to his heart. Markus didn't like feeling this vulnerable.

"Why don't you just get an assistant to buy them for you?"

Presley looked at him like he'd suddenly grown two heads. Mrs Barnett's was better described as what he would have expected if he'd stood up in church, farted, and then sat down again … during a funeral. *Actually, she'd probably have looked less horrified.*

"Well, bless your heart, but you haven't had a great deal of experience with Christmas, have you? Were you actually raised by wolves, or do you just act like it?" Mrs Barnett drawled, fingering the necklaces around her neck.

"Christmas is about giving on a personal level. Not having someone who doesn't even know the person pick it off the shelf for you. Seriously, I'm kinda with Mama on this one."

Markus's lips puckered in annoyance. They had no right to mock him for something they knew nothing about. And he sure as heck wasn't going to tell them anything about how he was raised. *It was going to be a long flight to Tennessee.*

HONESTLY, that man had the biggest ego of anyone she'd ever met. Suggesting having an employee picking out Christmas gifts for loved ones. She never could tell if he was serious or if he made comments like that to impress her. Thinking that he was treating her like one of his blonde floozies really got on her nerves. *Seriously, hadn't they gotten past all that nonsense? Was he really that insecure that he thought that was all he had to offer?* Maybe Markus needed this time on the farm more than she thought. He was about to get a crash course in humility and family— Barnett style.

Excitement made her smile out the window, giddy to be heading home. She was tired, so very tired, and it was just what the doctor ordered to recharge her batteries and see her family and Walter. She hoped Walter wouldn't be too upset that she'd brought a strange man home. *I'll cross that bridge when they meet.* There wasn't anything nicer than Christmastime on the farm. They'd get the fire going, and Daddy still hadn't gotten the Christmas tree. *Maybe that's the first thing Markus can help with to get him in the holiday mood.* Plotting her Christmas spirit makeover of Markus, she stared out the window. *He's not going to know what hit him.*

CHAPTER 15

FRANKLIN TENNESSEE, 10 DAYS BEFORE CHRISTMAS

*A*hh, *Nashville. Second only to Detroit on my list of places I've never wanted to go.* Markus kept his face neutral as their limo went through the city, past honky-tonks and places advertising hot chicken. Slowly, the urban sprawl released them into picturesque rolling hills and rivers, white post-and-rail fences with the obligatory cows and horses, stately homes and country stores. Markus wanted to gag at all the perfect greenery. *Give me bright lights and the ring of a poker machine any day.*

"Daddy was upset he couldn't pick us up from the airport, but he got called back to do another take of a song," Presley said, looking past him out the window. "We're almost there."

More uniform white fences, monotonous in their perfec-tion, and then the limo was turning into an asphalt drive, waiting for the large wrought iron gates to swing open before a house rose up in front of them. It was white—*argh, there's that color again*—with stately columns out the front and a porch. Markus did a double take at the porch swing. Large bay windows framed it on the lower level. It was big, but in no way as large a mansion that someone of Presley's caliber should own. It was ... homey. He turned to Presley in surprise.

She smiled at him, happiness and pride radiating from her. "It's great, isn't it? Welcome to the farm. Welcome to my home."

It was the reverence in which she spoke it—*home*—completely and perfectly at ease, tranquil. Markus felt envy wrap around his empty heart. He'd never once said the word like that, even when he'd been a kid. Then Presley turned her glowing eyes to him, giving a long sigh of contentment.

"It's good to be back."

The soft acceptance in her eyes soothed his vexed soul only to replace it with a yearning for something that was completely foreign to him. The longing for a home of his own.

Presley held the door open for the driver to bring their luggage in. Meanwhile, Markus took his coat off, looking around for someone to take it for him. "Well, bless your heart, if you want it hung, best be fixin' to hang it yourself." Mrs Barnett pointed to the closet near the main door. With a thoroughly unimpressed look, he complied.

Once safe to relinquish her post at the door, Presley divested herself of her own coat and followed suit. "Daddy has been waiting for us to come home before we put the decorations up and, of course, we still need to pick our Christmas tree."

"Why didn't you get the housekeeper to do it?" Markus

appeared to be waiting for staff of some description to make an appearance.

"Because we don't have one. We have a lady who comes once a week to clean the house, and because we're hardly ever here long enough to need someone to wait on us, that's it. Plus, it's not really the kind of people we are."

Markus looked like he was struggling to comprehend this strange parallel universe he now found himself in. "What about a gardener? Surely you don't do that yourself? Who looks after your animals—Walter?"

"Walter can barely look after himself. We look after the property and animals when we're here, which has been my father for the last little while, and when we're all away, my brother or sister will come up and care for them."

"Who picks up after them?" he pressed. Presley was confused why it seemed so important to him. It wasn't that big of a deal.

"We do." Markus sneered in disgust at her answer, his lip curling like he was smelling the pungent barnyard odors he was so fascinated with. "Now, let me show you to your room. You'll need to put some suitable clothes on. You"—she pointed at him—"and me are going to pick out a tree before the rest of the family come over and help decorate it."

"Are you serious?" A shadow of annoyance crossed his face.

Presley planted her hands on her hips, staring him down. "Yes, I really am. Remember? The deal was Christmas my way, and I'm holding you to it. Even if I have to drag you kicking and screaming."

"Unfortunately," he grumbled.

She smiled sweetly, patting him on the cheek. "Now, suga, just do what you're told, and who knows? Maybe if you stop bellyaching long enough, you might just enjoy yourself."

~

IF EVER THERE was a vision that summed up Markus's personal idea of hell, then surely he had found himself smack bang in the middle of it. Row upon row of Christmas trees stood in neat lines—small ones, large ones, enormous ones, thin ones, wide ones, triangle ones. A little girl barreled into Markus, almost taking his legs out and sending him crashing to the ground. Only some quick maneuvering saved his cashmere coat from getting caked in whatever it was he was walking on.

Huge brown eyes stared up at him from a face made sticky from the candy cane she sucked on. "Sorry, mister. Have you found your goldilocks yet?"

Markus gazed up ahead to where Presley was elbow-deep appraising a likely candidate for decorations. *Had he found his goldilocks? One with chestnut hair that crackled with fire?* "Kid, I don't know what you're talking about."

Brown eyes turned solemn, the mouth working away at the candy until she pulled it out with a plop. "You know, your goldilocks tree. Not too small, not too big, but just right."

A frazzled looking woman, a toddler on her hip, appeared. "I'm real sorry, I hope she wasn't bothering you. Susan, leave the nice man alone." She smiled apologetically up at him.

Nice man. The words stayed with Markus as he made his way to Presley. *What a dumb kid.* And then it hit him, wave after wave of painful memories. He'd been that dumb kid once, full to the brim with hope and Christmas cheer. Markus's chest tightened in a vicelike grip, the air no longer reaching his lungs. Blindly, he pushed his way past startled customers, branches clutching at his coat as if to trap him. Behind him he heard her "Markus," but he could not heed it any more than he could ask the wind to stop blowing.

Caught in his own torment, Markus knew that escape was all that mattered. Somehow, his feet brought him back to Presley's truck, his sides heaving as he threw up onto the pavement. And then a gentle hand was rubbing his back, murmuring that it was going to be all right.

Finally spent, he wiped his mouth with the tissue she offered him. Markus couldn't look at her, too afraid of what he would see there. Wordlessly, Presley held out a pack of breath mints. With a rueful smile, he accepted. Steeling himself, he raised his gaze to find soft concern in her glorious eyes.

"Do you want to talk about it?"

"Do I have a choice?"

"Yes. If you don't want to talk about it, I'm not going to pry. Whatever it is, it's something that only you can decide if you want to share it with me. But whatever you do decide, I want you to know that I'm here for you."

The breath mint helped, but the taste of bile was still bitter in his mouth. "It brought back some memories." Markus loathed the trembling in his voice.

"Not good ones?" Presley's hand was gentle on his arm.

"No, I've never been to a Christmas tree lot."

"Like, never? Where did you get your Christmas trees from?"

"We never had one." Memories of cold apartments at Christmastime, watching the other kids with their new toys and then—his mind shut down, refusing to delve deeper. Presley gave his arm a little squeeze, anchoring him back into the present.

"We don't have to do this if you don't want to. I can get my brother to pick one on his way over." Her voice had an infinitely compassionate tone.

"No, I can't go back in there." His voice broke. "But I can stay here with the truck. Go pick your tree."

"I think I spotted a winner when I was in there. Let me get the man to bundle it all up for us and then we can go. I promise I'll be quick."

Presley's eyes clung to his, gauging his reaction. A quick nod from him and she was on her way. True to her word, in a short time, the tree was safely loaded in the back of the truck and they were on their way. Markus slouched in the passenger seat, self-loathing and embarrassment his companion, no matter how much Presley tried to lighten the mood. It was a long drive back to the farm.

PRESLEY CLUTCHED THE STEERING WHEEL, fighting against the urge to pull the truck over and wrap Markus in her arms and smooth the wrinkles from his forehead and promise him that she would tame the demons he was fighting. She wondered what had happened in his childhood. Honestly, she'd kind of thought he'd hatched from an egg since he never mentioned family and was, well, such a stone-cold-hearted jerk all the time.

By the time they reached the farm, Markus had managed to retain some sort of equilibrium and was back to his controlled hard self. He was exceedingly polite, if distant, throughout introductions with her brother and sister and their families. When the decorations were brought down from the attic, Markus pleaded a headache. Presley watched him go, his expression haunted by things she could only guess at, and her heart broke.

The vibrant yellow yolks spilled over the puffy whites and mixed with the hollandaise sauce. *Nothing compares to Mama's eggs benedict made with eggs from our very own hens. Gosh, it was good to be home.*

"Are you fixin' to go up and check on Markus?" her daddy asked around a mouthful of bacon. "The man wasn't feeling well last night, and I'd be right torn up if he was lying in bed ill."

"I swear the man is just playing possum and doesn't want to face me after being rude and not helping with the decorating last night." Mama aggressively waved her spatula around, causing Presley to duck.

Presley was torn. Somehow it didn't seem right to share what had happened at the Christmas tree lot, and yet, she felt oddly protective of him and didn't want her mama to run his name down. "Mama, just let it be," she began.

"Well, looky what the cat dragged in," her mother interrupted, fixing the bleary-eyed Markus entering the room with a steely look. "Markus, I'll have you remember that you aren't in Vegas no more. If you want breakfast, I'd be fixin' to make sure you come down at a respectable hour."

"Mama, but you're still cooking yours," Presley protested.

"Leave the man alone," her daddy agreed. "Can't you see the poor man is suffering?" Daddy gave him a sympathetic smile. "I've been known to get a headache or two in my time as well. Comes with the territory with drumming. How're you feeling now?'

"A bit better till I got such a warm welcome here," Markus retorted in cold sarcasm.

"Aw, heck," Daddy muttered, Presley frantically trying to warn Markus with her eyes that he was in for it now.

"Well, bless your heart." Mama held a hand to her chest, her face the picture of outraged innocence. "Are you implying that I wasn't hospitable?"

"I wasn't implying. I was flat out saying it," Markus sneered.

"In our home, we keep respectable hours. Presley has already fed the horses and cleaned their stalls, and I've done the chickens. And all the while you were wallowing in your bed feeling sorry for yourself." Mrs Barnett slammed a plate of food in front of Markus. "Don't ever let it be said that I don't have good hospitality."

Markus muttered something dark and vaguely threatening under his breath as Mama pretended not to hear, instead contenting herself with glowering at him.

Presley rolled her eyes in exasperation at her daddy. "If you both are fixin' to be ornery, I'm going to go hang out with Walter."

Markus's head snapped up, his eyes dangerously narrowed to slits. "Is he here?"

"Of course he is. He lives here," Presley said.

"I think it's time me and this Walter met." Markus stood, boldly intimidating, his mouth tight and grim.

"Um, Walter isn't really a fan of meeting people," Presley tried to warn. The morning that had held such promise when she'd woken up had taken a serious turn for the worse.

"Tough. He's going to meet me." Markus stormed out of the door. Helplessly, Presley stared wide-eyed between her parents, unsure what to do. Sudden yelling and the sound of scrambling came from outside.

"You'd better go save him," Mrs Barnett said, her lips twitching suspiciously. "Mind you, there's no need to hurry."

Opening the door, Presley could only stare at the scene before her in amused wonder. Markus was pressed hard against the wall to her right, a large white goose flapping its wings at him and alternating between hissing and honking at him. Every time he so much as tried to inch away from the wall and make a hasty retreat through the open door, the goose attacked like a snapping pterodactyl.

"Shoo, Walter! That's not how we treat houseguests," admonished Presley. With one last snap at Markus's ankle, Walter strutted away, giving a series of pleased little honks.

"That's Walter?"

Presley pressed her hands to her mouth, desperately trying to contain her mirth that threatened to explode. The usually immaculate man had marks on his slacks that looked to be where he'd fallen over. He hastily righted himself, his hair sticking out on all angles and his eyes saucer wide.

"Yes, who did you think he was?"

She looked at him in bewilderment. Markus mulishly clamped his mouth shut, refusing to answer her. Slowly, it dawned on Presley. He'd somehow gotten it into his head that Walter was a man and he'd been … jealous? Giving up the fight, she let out a great whoop of laughter, clutching at her sides as she struggled to draw in air. Her mama and daddy appeared, taking in the sight of their mirth-riddled daughter and their disheveled houseguest and did the only thing they could do. They returned to their breakfast before it got cold, shaking their heads in disbelief.

~

Markus glared at Presley, giggles still convulsing her body. "That's it, I'm going back to civilization." He brushed past her into the house, stomping up to his room to change into fresh clothes and pack his things. *I knew it was a mistake to come here. It's not like Christmas has ever done me any favors.* Throwing a final silk tie in, he secured it and hauled it from the bed. *They can keep their farm and animals and stick it up their sweaters!*

His vent came to a screeching halt when he saw the grim faces of the Barnett's peering down at something on the table. Both Mr and Mrs Barnett had their arms around their ashen-faced daughter. "What's going on?"

Mr Barnett picked up an envelope and handed it to him. "This came in the mail. We were just opening it and then we came to this." Inside was a photo of Presley with her hand on his arm as he leaned against her truck, the Christmas tree lot in the background. Fury savaged his soul, causing him to crumple the image he held in his hand.

Mrs Barnett quickly retrieved it from him, turning it over. "There's more." On the other side, scrawled in red writing, was *I'm always close. Make sure you hang a stocking for me.*

Markus slammed his palms hard onto the table, causing everyone—already edgy—to jump, his anger becoming a scalding fury. "That's it, Presley. I'm calling Nate, and he's coming down here." He glared reproachfully at her parents. "I can't believe you don't have any security."

"Don't be ridiculous." Presley stirred uneasily in her chair. "It's Christmas. I don't want Nate to be away from his wife."

"Presley, I think you need to listen to him." Markus

threw his hands up in the air in mock surprise that someone had finally seen the light. "Listen to me," Mr Barnett said over his daughter and wife's protests. "From the first moment the nurse laid you in my arms, I swore to God that I would never let anything happen to you, and I ain't about to start now. This man"—he pointed to Markus—"all he's trying to do is protect you, and it's about time you let him."

Presley's vexation was clearly evident as she bit down hard on her bottom lip, her fingers drumming against her arm. "Fine," she huffed. "But before you go getting all smug about winning, I still need to buy the last of my Christmas presents. And since you want me to have protection so badly, looks like you're it."

A surge of pure testosterone flooded his body. A primal need that demanded to be satisfied. He almost hoped the stalker would reveal themselves, then he would make them pay for doing this to his woman.

Markus's eyebrows almost hit his hairline. Presley held her hand out to stall whatever it was that was going to come out of his mouth, already open and primed for some sort of snarky comment. "Don't. Whatever you're fixin' to say, I don't want to hear it." Snow was lightly falling outside the little curio store, but inside a fire crackled and vintage Christmas decorations gave it a cozy intimate feel.

"All I was going to say is that you can afford to buy people good gifts, you know, like a Rolex or Cartier bracelet." He picked up a beaded chakra necklace, holding it gingerly with the tip of one finger as though its cheapness would somehow taint him.

Dramatically, she put her palms to her head. "Oh my

gosh, you still don't get it, do you? It's about giving something that is special." *Why was he being so dense?*

Markus stabbed a finger at the unoffending jewelry. "That is not special."

"Yes, it is, because my sister-in-law loves things like that."

"I never would have guessed you were cheap, Presley Barnett." His mocking tone set her teeth on edge.

"I'm not cheap," she ground out.

"Yes, you are."

"Fine, what's your ultimate Christmas gift? What would you select for me?"

A dark, intense light gleamed out of his eyes as he smirked at her. "Something that only I could give you. Maybe the necklace that Richard Burton gifted Elizabeth Taylor, or a broach that Napoleon gave Josephine or"—he picked up a tendril of her hair, twisting it around his finger—"perhaps a guitar that Johnny Cash gave June Carter."

She closed her hand over his, so very conscious of how close he stood. His expensive aftershave delighted her senses almost as much as his nearness unsettled her in the most pleasant way. "Such overkill. For Christmas, I would be happy just to spend time with you—the real you."

Presley freed her hair and stepped back, breaking the spell. She tried not to giggle at the absurdly disgruntled look that marked his previously slick expression. *Oh, Markus. You still have so much to learn.* Plucking the much-maligned necklace up, she headed to the cashier to pay.

Leaving the shop, Presley cast discreet glances out of the corner of her eye. So far, she hadn't seen any traces of what had happened yesterday. The cute local shops had all of the best holiday season finery out, the porch rails and posts covered in garlands, large vintage mechanical snowmen and Santas, and enough lights to make a small child's dreams come true. If the Christmas tree lot had triggered such a severe reaction the previous day, surely this would have an impact on him.

"One more shop and I promise we're done shopping for the day." Presley pretended to not hear Markus's mutinous mutterings as she pushed open the door, setting the chimes to ringing. Inside was a riot of color, the small shop packed to overflowing with toys. "My nephew is the only one left to get a gift for," she said by way of explanation.

Idly, she wandered the rows, hoping inspiration would leap off the shelves. At last she decided on a miniature wood-working kit. *I'm sure Daddy will love showing him how it all works.* Satisfied, she went to find Markus. *It shouldn't be too difficult, after all, given the size of the shop.* Presley finally located him standing in front of a toy train set. It had been set up in a tiny Christmas landscape, the attention to detail mind-blowing. Markus stood, and for a moment, she caught a glimpse of him, unguarded, enthralled by the toy. *Was this what he'd been like as a child?*

Suddenly, as if feeling her gaze on him, his expression shuttered. "Have you finally managed to find something? How hard can it be to pick something for a little brat?"

And there's the jerk we all know and love. "Yes, I've been waiting for you actually." Presley gestured to the train set. "Unless there's something you want to buy?"

"I don't know what you mean." Markus huffed out of the store.

By now, the snow had stopped, but the chill still hung in the air. Out the front of a store in the parking lot, someone had set up a fire pit, complete with mismatched benches and chairs. "Oh." She grabbed his arm, childish excitement flaring. "You are so going to try this." Pulling a resistant Markus along, she headed over.

Taking a chair, she smiled around at the people already seated, rosy-cheeked from the warmth of the fire. A basket was passed to her, and she took several items out and handed it on to Markus. Doubtfully, he peered down into it. A brow quirked when he looked back at her. "Oh, come on. Everyone loves S'mores. I simply won't believe it if you tell me you don't like them."

The corners of his mouth twitched. "I don't hate them."

"Good."

Presley set to assembling her S'mores and holding it over the fire. Christmas carols wafted from the speakers that had been set up on the store's porch. Biting down on the chocolatey gooiness, she closed her eyes in contentment. *This is what life was about—a fire, good company, and food.* Presley opened her eyes to see Markus staring at her, his gaze intense and unfathomable.

"Now, this is living."

Markus licked his finger where some marshmallow had dribbled. For a moment, Presley forgot everything except for the sight of his tongue peeking out between his lips. "You could be forcing me to do worse things," he admitted. "Like shopping in junk stores." As he spoke, he glanced around almost continuously, a nervous tension to his body. "But if you're done, I think we should leave now."

"No, I thought we could enjoy ourselves here for a bit," Presley protested, disappointed that Markus wanted to go. Secretly, she'd been hoping that it would be a nice moment between the two of them.

"And I don't think it's safe for you to be out in the open like this."

Her skin began to crawl with the sensation she was being watched. Giving up, she popped the last piece of sugary goodness in her mouth and, with a final longing glance at the basket of ingredients that were still being passed around, stood, brushing her hands together. "Well, now that you've wrecked that for me, let's go," she huffed, pouting.

Markus reached out and caught her around the waist, pulling her close. "I'm not going to apologize for keeping you safe. Besides, you're adorable when you sulk." He touched her bottom lip lightly with his thumb, causing shivers to dance deliciously down her spine. "Now, let's go."

Arm still snagged around her, he marched off, taking her with him. For once, Presley didn't argue, her knees too weak from his commanding presence to fight. *Maybe sometimes it's nice to lose after all.*

～

"You want to do what!?" exploded Markus. How could such a beautiful, intelligent woman be so stubborn?

"I don't want to, I am," Presley corrected, making herself a cup of hot cocoa.

"No, absolutely not. Mr Barnett, talk some sense into your daughter."

"Presley, I don't think it's a good idea," Mr Barnett said.

"Daddy, you know how much I love this movie. I'm going." She poked her tongue out at Markus. He almost returned the gesture, barely catching himself in time from sinking to her childish level.

"Nate, are you just going to hide in the corner? If you are, I'm not sure you were worth the effort to fly out on my plane. You could've just come commercial." Markus glowered at the big man who was balancing a plate of home-made sugar cookies on his lap while he drunk his hot cocoa.

"I believe I'll be able to sufficiently keep Presley safe in a controlled environment like that. And of course, I'll take all necessary precautions." Markus felt a nerve in his jaw twitch to life at the other man's calm assurance. *When this is all over, I'm going to get a new head of security.*

"Fine, but it better be a good movie." Markus ground the words out from between clenched teeth.

"It's *Miracle on 34th Street*," Presley said as though that explained everything. Markus stared blankly at her.

"It's a Christmas classic," Nate helpfully supplied.

"Just sit there and eat your cookies," Markus said, putting one into his own mouth in defeat.

The theater was full of people, enough to make Markus's heart beat faster and perspiration break out on his forehead. "I'll have two popcorns and sodas," he said to the attendant.

"Three," Presley held her fingers up.

"If you think I'm buying popcorn for him, you've got another thing coming." Markus sighed in defeat. "Three."

Nate guided them to the back row of the theater, making sure no one would be behind them, and placed her securely between both men. As the opening credits rolled, Markus found himself gazing at her profile as she stared transfixed at the big screen, the images casting shadows over her face. Slowly, he stretched his arm until it was around her, and Presley snuggled into him. *Maybe this wasn't such a bad idea, after all.* A feeling of being in complete harmony with the woman beside him washed over him. Could it always be like this? The fiery arguments giving spice and then the cooling balm of just being together?

Much later after Nate had secured the house, Markus found himself pouring a cup of cocoa, not yet ready for sleep.

"Do you mind if I join you?" Presley asked softly, a snuggly looking cowhide print robe and slippers in place.

"It's your house." Regardless of his words, he was happy she'd come down and he made her a cup.

"I wanted to thank you for coming to the movies with me tonight."

"I was under the impression you were going to go

whether I went or not. In fact, I think you and Nate would have had a great time," he groused.

Presley giggled into her mug. "Who knew Nate was such a fan of Christmas movies?"

"I'm beginning to think I need to do better employee background checks."

"I think it's cute."

"You would." Silence, warm and comfortable, stretched between them. And something else, fragile and tentative, different to the sparks that usually flew between them.

"Markus?" Presley's voice was softly tentative through the happy haze.

"Yes?"

"Yesterday, at the Christmas tree lot, what happened?"

Markus stiffened, filled with burning humiliation and shame. "I thought I said I didn't want to talk about it." His voice was caustic.

Presley dropped her eyes, staring pink-cheeked down into the mug, suitably chastised. "You did."

He felt like he was standing on the edge of a great abyss, the ground giving way beneath. But to step off the edge meant falling into the darkness he'd spent his entire adult life pulling himself out of. Markus raked shaking hands through his hair. *If I do, will she look at me differently?* Or would his brightly shining, fiery angel be able to chase the shadows away?

"I've always hated Christmas."

"Even as a kid?"

"Especially as a kid." The words were flat and final.

"Oh." This time the silence that stretched between them was tense, uneasy.

Before he could change his mind, the words began to tumble from his mouth. "My mom was an addict and we were poor. Like, dirt-poor people seemed rich to me as a kid." He swallowed, the memories clawing at him, knowing how the story ended. "And then one Christmas, she promised me a visit to a Christmas tree lot. She gave me a candy cane. I don't know where she got it from, we'd never had money for that before. And she told me to go look at the trees. Turns out she was meeting with her drug dealer. I spent ages trying to find her."

The memory of crying, strangers looking at him and then away as though not wanting to get involved until an elderly couple had stopped, the old man kneeling down on arthritic knees until his kindly face had been level with his and asked what was wrong. He promised they would find his mom. And they'd found his mom all right.

"She couldn't resist sampling what she'd bought and had gone back to the car. The stuff must have been purer that time. Her body was already cold by the time the paramedics were called. After that I bounced around from foster care to foster care. Some bad, and others that made the bad ones seem good."

"Markus, I had no idea." Presley lifted her eyes, shimmering with unshed tears as she walked over, gently brushing the hair from his eyes. She wrapped her arms around him and pulled him into her, like she could somehow absorb the humiliation and sorrow from his very bones. Markus stiffly resisted. "I want you to know this and really hear it when I say it to you. There's nothing you can tell me or show me about you that would scare me away. I've cared about you even when you were a jerk, and I'm not fixin' to go anywhere now. You will never be alone again."

The dam holding the great darkness at bay broke, and he sobbed brokenly into her tender arms. *Never alone again.*

The phone vibrated on the kitchen table. Presley wiped her hands carefully on the tea towel that Markus held out for her before answering it. "Hello?"

"Hello, Presley, it's Paul. I hope you're having a good break on the farm."

She smiled over to where Markus and Nate stood with her mama as she tried her best to teach them how to make her famous biscuits, made slightly comical by the cast on her arm. "Yeah, I think this is exactly what I needed."

"Good, good. Well, I have everything under control here. In fact, your first show back is sold out and the waiting list is full, too." Paul paused, and Presley wondered idly if he was congratulating himself or if she should. "Now, what I called about was I'm thinking about coming down to Nashville in a few days' time and maybe we could catch up? With everything that happened, I never did manage to give you my Christmas gift."

"Um, well I'm the guest of honor for the Christmas carols here on Christmas Eve, but other than that, I don't have any firm plans."

"Excellent. I'll sure up my plans and let you know."

Presley hung up the phone and went and wrapped her arms around a slightly floury Markus. "Paul says he has everything under control."

"He should. It's what I pay him for," Markus grumbled.

"Well, I'm going to head out and feed up the animals."

"If I'm almost finished here, I'll come help you." Presley was shocked when Markus looked askance at her mother.

"All that's left is to put them in the oven," Mama declared, picking bits of dough from her fingers.

"Now, don't be offering if you don't mean it," Presley warned, wagging her finger playfully at him.

"I mean it."

"Even if it means picking up manure?"

Markus wrinkled his nose. "Even if it means that."

"Well, in that case, you'd better come with me. There's something I want to give you first."

There was a slight hesitation in his crystal eyes. "Should I be scared?"

"No." She grabbed his hand and pulled his resisting body out to where the Christmas tree stood, retrieving several packages from underneath. "I got these for you for Christmas, but I think you're going to need them now." When he shoved his hands behind his back so as not to touch the gifts, she laughed. "Don't worry, there's a few more for you under there."

Sitting down, a bewildered expression on his face, he opened the paper to reveal a pair of brown cowboy boots and a sand-colored Stetson. "You got me cowboy clothes?"

"Yep. If you're fixin' to help out on the farm, best you look the part."

Markus quickly put them on and stood up for her inspection. "How do I look?"

"Like a proper cowboy." *An especially hot cowboy.* "Now, let's go shovel some manure."

"Can't wait," Markus retorted dryly. "Really, I could wait, you know, just in case you had some things you needed to do first."

Resorting to her previous tactic, she grabbed his hand and dragged him out to the barn.

Half an hour later, Presley wiped her forehead with the back of her hand. Maybe she should have gotten Markus to clean the barn earlier. Sure, he hadn't magically turned into a sweetheart, but the hard edges had gotten softer. In one of the stalls, she could hear him muttering at Walter. The fact he'd even offered to tend to the goose had shocked her. Leaning on her fork, she strained her ears to catch what he was saying.

"I hear, in some countries, that before turkey was all the rage for Christmas, they ate goose. Maybe we should go back to the old ways."

"Markus!" Presley snorted with laughter.

"Hey, this is a private conversation between me and Walter."

"Well, when you're finished your private conversation, I think it's time to head back to the house and clean up. Those biscuits should be ready, and Mama will have made gravy for it too."

"You had me at biscuits," he said, falling in step beside her. Maybe her Operation Christmas Spirit was starting to work.

PRESLEY GRINNED at Markus as she pushed open the door, the smile sliding off her face at the tense scene at the kitchen table. Nate and her parents sat grimly, casting anxious glances between them.

"Someone better start talking." Steel ran through Markus's voice. "Nate." He jerked his chin at his security man commandingly.

"Another parcel has arrived." The security manager gestured to the stocking that was on the table. Presley inched forward, her hand hovering hesitantly over it as though afraid to touch it.

"Leave it," Markus ordered. "I'll do it." He reached down and peered inside. It was stuffed full of pictures. He upended it and they came cascading out onto the table. Pictures of her at The Chimera, getting on his private plane, them talking at Halloween, backstage at her show, and finally, them sitting beside a firepit having S'mores. Markus's heart stopped beating. "That's it. You're canceling your show."

"No."

"There's more, Markus." Nate picked up the box it had come in. The post mark was Nashville.

"Ah, heck no." Markus grabbed her by the arms, staring into her eyes, her pupils dilated, willing her to see sense. "Presley, this is serious. You're canceling."

Her eyes narrowed, spitting fire at him. "That's not your call to make."

Frustration—or was it fear?—made his voice rough. "Someone talk some sense into her."

"Maybe we should think about this," Mr Barnett said, glancing at his wife.

"Presley's right, there's no need to cancel anything. Security will be tight, and I doubt the stalker will do anything with so many people around. Plus, we'll all be there backstage as well. I'm sure we can keep her safe."

Markus released Presley. "I hope you all don't live to regret this." Not trusting himself to utter another word, he stormed from the room.

Sitting on his bed, staring out the window to the pond

that lay beyond, he felt impotent at his lack of ability to make them see how very real the danger was to Presley.

The door made a soft groan as it opened. *I'm not turning around. They can go away.* Quiet footsteps padded on the floorboards, a shadow falling across him before the mattress sunk down beside him.

"I brought you a cup of eggnog." Presley's voice was low and smooth as she held the cup out to him. "It's Mama's secret recipe."

Glancing down at the cup, he took it, taking a grudging sip. Warmth flowed down his throat, the creamy liquid packing quite a bourbon punch. *Wow, Mrs Barnett sure liked her eggnog strong.* Taking another bracing drink, he finally looked at Presley. "It's such a stupid idea to perform, knowing that they're out there. Don't even get me started on your parents supporting you in this idiocy."

There was a pensive shimmer in the shadow of Presley's eyes. *Maybe I'm finally getting through to her.* "This is who I am. I'm a performer. It's not the first stalker I've ever had, and it probably won't be the last. Mama thought she was keeping them all secret from me, but I always knew deep down." She rested her hand lightly on his thigh. Markus's hand came down possessively over the top of it. "I truly believe I was put here on God's green earth to perform and make people happy. And what better way to do that than by sharing the Christmas spirit and singing carols? Being on stage makes my soul happy." Her eyes glistened with emotion.

Markus felt the nauseating sinking of despair, knowing that he'd failed, that no matter what he said, she was still going to go on that stage. "It's hard to have a happy soul when you're dead."

"Even dead people have happy souls because of how they've lived their lives."

Presley rested her head against his shoulder, and he

wrapped his free arm tightly around her as though he could keep her beside him forever. Sitting there, staring out at the peaceful view of what Mrs Barnett constantly referred to as God's country, Markus wondered if his mom had died with a happy soul. All he knew was that the world needed the joy that Presley brought it—as long as she kept her promise. That he'd never be alone again.

Markus's muscles were rigid with adrenaline and nerves, his gaze constantly scanning everyone and everything. The man laying cable—could it be him? The lady shepherding the little darlings of the choir who would sing on stage with Presley—what better disguise? And it was only the sound check and dress rehearsal for tomorrow night's carols. Was his heart going to hold up to the stress, or expire before the main event ever happened? Presley beamed at him as she made her way over. The relief that Presley had stepped off the stage and was now headed to the relative safety of the wings was short-lived.

"Paul," she cried happily, giving him a quick hug. "You never did get back to me with when you were coming."

Mrs Barnett bustled over. "Paul, it does my heart good to see you." Her delight evident, she enveloped him into a hug that rivaled her daughter's. "How long you fixin' to be here?"

"I'm only here for a few days. In fact, I fly out the morning after your carols."

"Well, you must come for a late supper at the farm

tomorrow night. It's a family tradition. For as long as a Barnett has sung at these carols, we've been having late suppers. And I can tell you, there have been a lot of musically inclined Barnett's."

Markus wanted to gag. Did Mrs Barnett have to lay it on so thick? Sure, the guy seemed nice enough, but to invite him for dinner? Who wanted to spend more time with someone they worked with?

Paul patted Mrs Barnett on the hand, his happy face flushed. "It would be my pleasure." The PR manager finally looked up to see Mr Barnett and Markus glowering at him. For some reason, Markus got the distinct impression that the older man wasn't much of a fan of Paul's. "Mr Barnett, it's so nice to meet you again." Paul extended a hand to Presley's father.

Mr Barnett stared down at it, hesitating a moment longer than was strictly good manners before clasping it. "What brings you to Tennessee?"

The curt way Presley's dad cut to the chase made Markus feel quite fond of the old man. Red crept up Paul's neck, blossoming onto his face, and he hastily extracted his hand. "I'm here on business."

His answer piqued Markus's interest. "What business? I don't remember there being anything you needed to do down here for The Chimera?"

"Oh, it's not for the casino," Paul stammered, his fingers playing with the cuff of his shirt. "An opportunity has come up to invest in a business down here and I thought I'd check it out. You know, something for my retirement."

Markus gave the other man a brutal and unfriendly glare. "As long as it doesn't impact on your work at my casino, I don't care what you do. If it does, you might be heading for retirement faster than you'd anticipated."

"Markus." Presley's voice was horrified as she tapped him lightly on the arm. "Leave the poor man alone."

Mrs Barnett linked her arm with Paul's. "Now, you simply must tell me all the gossip that's happened since we've been gone." With a final reproachful glare at Markus, Presley followed.

He didn't understand what they saw in that toad of a man. Mr Barnett patted his shoulder. "My bet's on you," he said before trailing off after them, no doubt to keep an eye on his wife. Markus was left pondering why, exactly, the old man thought there was any other option.

STANDING in the wings of the stage, it felt surreal. Presley had practically grown up on it, performing every Christmas. But now, standing here in the same outfit she'd worn for her Christmas concert at The Chimera, a suffocating weight pressed down on her.

"Hey, are you feeling all right? If you're not, let's cancel and get you home."

Presley turned to give Markus a narrow-eyed glare. "I'm not canceling. I'm fine."

Markus looked like he didn't quite believe her but satisfied himself with casting a roving eye over her outfit. A flash of recognition fired in his eyes. "Isn't that the same one you wore to hospital?"

Trust him to say it like that. "If by that you mean is this the one I wore at The Chimera, then yes, it is."

"And you don't think that's asking for trouble at all?" Gosh, she hated the patronizing way he said it, his brows raised in the air like she was a simpleton.

"No. In fact, I think that it will bring me good luck. I love the color and how it moves around me. It puts me in the Christmas spirit."

"It put you in hospital last time."

"A snowman put me in hospital last time."

Markus pretended to look on stage where an elderly choir was singing. "Don't tell me he's here, too?"

"You know full well that prop isn't here," Presley snapped out before she could stop it. "Argh, why are you being such a jerk?" She turned away with her hands clenched tightly at her sides. She didn't need this right now.

Markus halted her escape with a firm hand on her elbow. If his touch halted her departure, his next words rooted her to the spot. "Because I'm scared. And I'm frustrated that no one will listen to me."

Presley turned and found herself pulled into protective arms. "I promise nothing will happen."

"You've already made me one promise that doesn't look like you're taking too seriously," he murmured against her ear.

Presley jerked back. "That you'll never be alone? Of course I take that seriously."

"Then prove it. Walk out of here with me. Let's go back to the farm. Heck, let's go anywhere. I don't care, as long as you're safe," Markus pleaded in a harsh, raw voice.

She stared wordlessly at him, her heart pounding. The tenderness in his expression amazed her. Presley fought against the uncertainty his impassioned speech had aroused in her.

"Here's your mic pack." Mrs Barnett appeared from the abyss of the backstage area. With deft movements, she secured it and propelled her daughter forward as her name was introduced to the crowd. With a lingering look over her shoulder asking for forgiveness, Presley stepped out onto the stage.

From her vantage looking down at the people, she could make out a sea of faces, some in Christmas sweaters, others in Santa hats and elf ears. And for the first time, real fear grabbed hold of her. Any one of them out there in that faceless crowd could be her stalker, waiting, always there. As the music swelled, she lifted her mic.

I'm a performer, this is what I do. She opened her mouth and sang as though her heart would burst. The carol was one she'd always loved—*O Holy Night*—and on this night, as she sang with an orchestra for backing, she imagined the original holy night and belief burned brightly through her.

As the last notes died away, she blew a kiss to the thunderous rapture of the crowd and walked off. Markus looked like he was caught in some sort of enchantment, his eyes wide and slightly glazed as he stared back at her. The hardness that usually lined his eyes were softened and, in that moment, Presley felt what was between them deepen. She took both of his hands and smiled, putting her heart into her eyes. Tentatively, this new vulnerable Markus returned it. Somehow Presley had fallen in love with this complicated, prickly as a porcupine man and she couldn't be happier.

"Come on, child, you're gonna catch a cold standing there in that costume." Mrs Barnett bustled in and hurried her daughter away. Presley looked over her shoulder and smiled at Markus ruefully. He gave her a helpless little shrug as if to say it didn't matter, they had all the time in the world.

It would have to be one of the quickest wardrobe changes she'd ever done in her career. Presley was dressed in jeans and a thick sweater in no time at all, her mama gathering up the discarded costumes.

"I'll get these hung up, then I'll meet you out with Daddy and Markus." Her eyes sparkled. "I'm sure you're fixin' to get right back to him."

Presley knew she must look like some kind of lovestruck

fool, but she couldn't help it. It felt like her soul was light as a feather and glowing with contentment, her heart fit to over-flow. Her mama chucked her under the chin.

"You don't need to say a word. I remember what it was like when I first fell in love with your daddy. And I have a little secret—it only gets better." As her mama walked out of the room, Presley couldn't imagine how it could possibly get better than how she felt now.

"Your performance was sublime," Paul said by way of greeting as he strolled into the room, looking comical in his over-the-top Christmas sweater.

"Oh, Paul, I love how much you've gotten into the holiday spirit." She giggled. "And thanks, it was better than the last time I performed. I wanted to tell you how much I appreci-ated you smoothing all of that over for me."

Paul waved his hand dismissively in the air. "I would do anything for you."

"Well, I would never ask you to do more than your job."

He picked a piece of lint from his coat that was draped over his arm. "Besides to see your stellar performance, I really only came to give you my Christmas gift. It's out in my car, but it's a bit too bulky to carry through a crowded back-stage area. Is it okay if you come out to get it and we can put it straight into your car?" he suggested, his hand stopping its restless stroking of the fabric.

"Of course, Paul. But you really didn't need to go to any bother for me. Just let me get my coat and find Nate." Strangely, when they stepped out into the corridor, Nate wasn't there as anticipated. "Oh, well, I guess we should wait until he comes back."

Paul smiled indulgently at her. "The poor man is probably getting himself something to eat." He put his hand on his chest, over his heart. "But I promise I will keep you safe and allow no ill to befall you."

Presley giggled at his gallant gesture and, reassured, tucked her arm into his. "Well then, what more could a gal ask for?"

An intense gleam flickered in his eyes. "What more, indeed."

CHAPTER 19

He knew he hadn't imagined that moment with Presley. Markus's heart swelled with an emotion he'd thought long dead, and he found himself smiling at random people passing by as he stood beside Mr Barnett waiting. Some even gave him a tentative smile in return.

"You know, you don't have to try and impress Presley all the time. Money, power, fame, none of it matters to her and it never has. She has a good heart, and she's intuitive. She'll see who you are long before you even do." Mr Barnett looked at Markus with wise eyes. "Have you told her yet?"

"Told her what?" There was something about the calmness that radiated from the older man that Markus found soothing. Strangely, he was one of the few people he could ever remember having time for.

"Son, I'm old, not blind or stupid." Mr Barnett continued to pierce into his soul with his gaze. "That you're in love with her."

Markus was the first to drop eye contact. "I'm more of a love 'em and leave 'em type of guy." He tried to depict a casual ease he didn't feel.

The old man gave a humph. "Not anymore. And take it from someone who's seen this kinda thing before. You've got it bad. For what it's worth, I think you're the type of man Presley needs. She wears her heart on her sleeve and believes the best in everyone, but I worry about her, and you're a jerk."

"Thanks." Markus wasn't sure if he liked where this was going.

Mr Barnett's eyes twinkled merrily. "It's that jaded view of the world that'll keep her safe. I know that you will protect her and her heart with your life. I guess what I'm trying to say is that you have my blessing for a happy life with my daughter."

Markus almost blurted out that he didn't need anyone's blessing to do anything, but suddenly the words penetrated his armor. The acceptance that he was being offered brought with it a measure of humility. This father, who clearly loved his daughter, thought he was the right man to cherish her. Markus swallowed the lump that formed in his throat. Uncomfortable with the emotions buffeting him, he made a show of glancing at his watch. *What on earth was keeping Presley?*

~

"You know, you're in for a real treat tonight. Mama makes the best food for her late-night supper. She's fixin' to have pies and her biscuits and gravy and ham and much more." Presley held her hands expansively wide for emphasis.

"I can't begin to tell you how much I'm looking forward to later tonight." For a moment, the shadows made Paul's familiar face look eerily like it belonged to someone else. Presley shook the outlandish notion from her head.

"You never did tell us what your plans are for Christmas

day. Surely you're not fixin' to fly out and spend it alone." Presley almost slid on a piece of slick pavement but was saved by Paul's tight grip on her arm. She smiled her gratitude up at him.

"No, I won't be alone. And this year, I think it will be particularly memorable." Paul's eyes were hooded, and Presley thought maybe he was being coy about seeing someone. Strange that he'd never mentioned it before, but maybe he didn't talk about relationships at work. His teeth flashed in his shadowy face. "We're almost there now, and then I know everything will have been worth it."

Presley thought of the tie she had under the Christmas tree for him. *Now I wish I'd gotten that platinum fountain pen as well. Dang, I hope he hasn't gone to too much effort.* Chewing on the inside of her mouth unhappily, she followed where he led her into the night.

Mrs Barnett waited for an elf and a sugar plum fairy to pass by before making her way over to the menfolk, her handbag over her arm. Mouth pursed, she made a show of looking around her. "I thought Presley would be out by now."

There was something about her casual utterance that made Markus's heart rate spike. Quickly, his long strides ate up the distance to Presley's empty dressing room.

"Well, she can't be too far. And it looks like Nate is with her." Mrs Barnett gave him a pointed look. "But if it makes everyone feel better, I'll give her phone a call."

It was only through a superior use of willpower that Markus didn't know he possessed that stopped him from giving the woman a piece of his mind. Slowly, he watched her smugly mocking expression turn worried, her brow furrowing into deep crevasses, eyes haunted.

"She's not answering."

Markus yanked his phone out of his pocket, stabbing at the screen, fit to put his finger through it. "If you know what's good for you, you better answer your phone, Nate," he muttered darkly.

"Wait, can you hear that?' Mr Barnett held his hand up for quiet.

Markus strained forward, every nerve tight as he tried to listen. "There," he cried in triumph, pointing to a dark side corridor that was being used to store props.

Charging forward, he left the Barnett's in his wake. The ringing got louder until he was almost to the end. Several candy canes, large fake pumpkins and a pot of gold had been piled haphazardly, and it was from beneath this holiday jumble that Nate's phone continued to ring.

"Help me move this stuff," Markus commanded. Mr Barnett put his spritely drummer's arms into action, yanking props off the pile and throwing them into a heap behind him.

It only took the removal of a few pieces before Nate's prone form emerged. "Oh, the blessed saints." Mrs Barnett held a shaky hand to her mouth as Markus knelt to check for signs of life. "Is it..." The words trailed off as though speaking them aloud would somehow curse the man.

Desperately Markus sought a pulse. *There.* Jubilant relief made him dizzy, forcing him to close his eyes. "He's alive." Panic clamped its shadowy fist around his heart, twisting it into knots. *If Nate's here, where's Presley?* He stood abruptly, almost causing a pumpkin to topple back on the unconscious man. "I'm going to find Presley."

"Markus?" Mrs Barnett's voice was shaky, fear sending tremors through it. He didn't have time for this right now. Self-righteous anger made him glare at her. *This was all her fault. If they'd canceled, this wouldn't be happening.* Mrs Barnett lifted grief-stricken eyes to meet his accusing ones. "I'll stay with Nate. You go bring back my daughter to me." It was as close to an apology as he was ever going to get from her. Markus gave a tight nod and then bounded away.

~

THE NOISE from the crowd had faded to a barely audible din as Paul led Presley onward. It was with a sense of relief that he finally gestured at the car parked in the dimly lit alley. "I'm sorry it's all this way, but with the crowds, it was the best I could do and honestly, I wouldn't have even found it if I hadn't gotten lost looking for a park in the first place," Paul said in a great gush of words.

Presley pulled her coat tighter around her, snow starting to lightly fall. Where normally it would enthrall her with its bright purity, here in the dingy alley, it felt dark and dirty. A shiver ran up her spine, sending goosebumps erupting out over her arms. "I don't think I've ever been down here before."

"I don't think a lot of people know about it." Paul agreed, the lights of the car unlocking seemed overly bright, out of place in a landscape of shadows. He opened the back passenger door wide. In the reflected interior light, his eyes gleamed. Suddenly, the light flickered and went out. "Dang it, I think the bulb just blew. Talk about crumby timing."

A flicker of apprehension went through her. "Maybe we should go back and get a torch or something." Her voice was shakier than she would have liked.

"No, we've come all this way. I'll hold my phone up and you can shimmy in and get it."

Presley swallowed and found her voice with difficulty, her stomach churning with anxiety and a nameless fear, aware that Paul had moved to position himself slightly behind her. "Why do I have to go in the car? Surely it would be better for you to," she stalled.

"Darn, Presley, why are you making this hard?" His voice, though quiet, had an ominous quality. "Just get in the car."

"No." Presley swung around wildly, her gut demanding she flee. Her eyes widened at the gun she found herself staring at. "What are you doing, Paul?" Sheer, black fright engulfed her.

"Get in the car," Paul repeated, each word chilling in its quietness.

A quick and disturbing thought forced its way into Presley's brain. *If I get into that car, something bad is going to happen to me.* "Why did you do it?"

"Ah, I see you've figured it out," he said, his voice softly mocking. "I must say, I was a little disappointed you didn't earlier, but then a slight flaw only serves to highlight the perfection of the rest."

Presley searched anxiously for the meaning behind the words. At a loss, she decided that the longer she could keep him talking, the better chance she had of coming out of this situation alive. "But why did you do it at all? Were you stalking me before you started working at The Chimera?"

"I was never a stalker. It was always about the music for me. Your mother's voice called to me, and then she gave it all away for you." He wagged a finger in her face like she was a naughty child. "But when I heard your voice, I'd never heard anything so pure in my life. I knew then what I had to do. The job was a complete coincidence, but one I was hardly going to pass on."

Presley's head swam. Nothing was making sense. "Then why did you start sending me the pictures?"

"You needed to stay pure." Paul's voice became shrill. "How could you make the music if you weren't pure anymore?" He began to pace, all the while keeping the gun trained on her. "Markus was going to sully you, corrupt everything that was good about you." Paul stopped and stared intently at her. "Don't you see? I couldn't let that happen, I can't," he quickly corrected himself. "That's why I'm making sure he never gets near you again. But it's more than that. I'm going to make sure nothing like that can happen ever again."

The ferocity of his demented passion was frightening. "What does that mean?"

"I'm going to take you somewhere safe, away from the filth in this world."

Icy fear clutched at her heart as he stepped closer, gun pointed to her chest.

THE ALLEY SMELLED of decay and abandonment, the snow adding to the dank odor. Surely Presley hadn't come this way. But something tugged at Markus, urging him onward when logic told him to turn back. *Maybe she didn't come of her own free will.* For a moment, the fear paralyzed him so that even his heart seemed to stop.

Further into the shadows, he suddenly heard a sharp, fear-filled "NO!" screamed out and the sound of a scuffle. A very sharp, loud crack rent the air, and with it, taking all the oxygen from Markus's lungs. The sound of his heartbeat thrashed in his ears, and he shot forward, blind to anything but that single cry from Presley. His breath coming out in ragged, gasping breaths, he rounded the corner, horror making his limbs go weak. Paul stood over a sobbing Presley crumpled on the ground. In the poor lighting, it was impossible to see if she'd been hit or not. Shock yielded quickly to fury. He was going to kill Paul and he was going to enjoy it.

"I never did like you." Markus threw the words at Paul like stones.

The whites of Paul's eyes glinted at him like a feral rat coming up from the sewer. "You keep your evil away from her. You've tarnished her enough." He bared his teeth at him. *Make that a rabid, feral sewer rat.*

"There's only one person here who's evil." Presley spat her loathing at him. Pride for her bravery warred with anger at her stupidity as Paul swung his attention back to her. Not stupid. Smart. *My smart, brave cowgirl.*

Seeing his opportunity, Markus rushed forward. Hearing his charge at the last moment, Paul swung the gun around and got a shot off. Pain blossomed through Markus's shoulder, but now driven berserk by the heady combination of adrenaline, rage, and fierce protectiveness, he relentlessly plowed into the deranged Marketing Manager. The force of his momentum knocked both of them off their feet, the gun flying across the moldy concrete. Markus, the first to recover, smashed his fist into his foe's face. Paul, with the superhuman strength of the insane, managed to roll Markus onto his back, the positions now reversed.

A shot rang out, dangerously close. "Get off him, Paul." Hysteria shook through each word Presley screamed. Markus pulled himself free from underneath Paul, gingerly holding his shoulder as he made his way over to her. Her hands shook uncontrollably as sobs racked her body, but still she kept the gun trained on Paul.

"It's no small thing to take a life," Markus said with quiet emphasis. "If you do this, you can't undo it."

"It was him. All that time, he watched me and pretended to be my friend. I trusted him." Presley's breathing came out in short, erratic sob-filled gasps.

"I know, but he was right about one thing. I'm tarnished. Let me take care of this."

He reached a hand out, the barrel of the gun burning against his palm. "Let this be the one thing I can give you." Presley remained unmoving for a heartbeat longer as though fighting an internal battle before allowing him to pry it from her cold fingers. His soul shattered as she seemed to crumple once the firearm had been removed.

Markus's shoulder was beginning to throb, pain shooting down his arm as he walked over to the still defiant Paul. Great waves of agony seemed to make the world go dull. "So you're going to kill me?" snarled the demented man.

"I should for what you did to Presley and what you would've done if you hadn't been stopped. But you're not worth the jail time which, believe me, you're going to have a long time to appreciate for yourself." Markus hauled his uninjured arm back and let fly, landing a resounding blow to Paul's jaw. The other man's eyes rolled back into his head and he dropped motionless to the ground. Markus's last thought as his legs buckled and the ground rushed up to meet him was, *Look at me with my personal growth and all. Presley must be rubbing off on me.* And then nothing.

GROGGILY, Markus became aware his head was cradled by something soft and warm, a tender hand brushing his brow. He felt like he was sinking in quicksand, the world fading again. *Just a moment longer, Mom, and I swear I'll get up.*

"It looks like he's coming around again," Mr Barnett said. Markus opened his eyes to find that he lay in Presley's lap. The painful throbbing in his shoulder didn't appear to be part of some dastardly dream and had, in fact, followed him back to consciousness. Mr Barnett was holding what looked to be a lacy handkerchief to it.

Slowly rolling his head from side to side, Markus made a

move to sit up. "Steady, son." Mr Barnett put a restraining hand on his chest and, as feeble as a kitten, Markus found he couldn't resist the gentle pressure to lay back down again. "You've lost a lot of blood."

Presley leaned forward and placed a tender kiss on his brow. "It's going to be okay. I promise I won't leave you alone." She managed a tremulous smile. Her hand clasped his tightly like she was trying to give him some of her strength.

Head lolling to the side, he was darkly amused to see Mrs Barnett giving glowering glares at the restrained Paul. If Markus wasn't mistaken, it looked like they'd used Mrs Barnett's candy cane striped scarf to do it. Beside the prisoner, Nate held a hand to his temple. A surprising shot of relief went through Markus that the stoic security manager had escaped relatively unharmed.

In the distance, he could hear sirens approaching as shivers began to rack his body. Finally giving into the fatigue and trauma, he closed his eyes, drifting off to the tender administrations of his woman. *I'm safe. She won't ever let me be alone again.*

CHAPTER 20

The nurse checking Markus's blood pressure was wearing a pair of reindeer antlers. There was no denying that this Christmas had shaped up to be unlike anything he'd ever experienced, and it was only Christmas Eve. It might be all the drugs he had coursing through his system, but suddenly he got it. Standing on the other side of his bed, holding his hand like she planned on never letting go again—which she hadn't, except for when the doctors had had to forcibly remove her to check him over when he was brought into emergency—was truly the one thing of value he possessed in his life. And she was priceless.

His gaze on her, she returned his look with heartrending tenderness. Blackness lashed at his soul when he thought of how close he'd come to losing her. "Presley, if something had happened…" he began.

Presley pressed a gentle finger to his lips, silencing him. "Shh. But it didn't. I promised you that you will never be alone again, and I meant it."

The nurse, satisfied, released the cuff and made a quick note before leaving. Mr and Mrs Barnett stood in the corner of the room with a ragged-looking Nate. A check over had revealed that except for a headache and his wounded pride, he was none the worse for his run in with the Christmas props. Idly, Markus wondered how much mileage he'd get from Nate by holding it over his head that he'd tell everyone back at The Chimera. He pursed his lips. Somehow, he didn't think Presley would like him doing it. *Maybe I could be sneaky about it. She'd never have to know...*

Mr Barnett cleared his throat. "I think we should give the kids some alone time." *Gosh, I knew there was a reason I liked that old man.* "Anyway, we still need to go home and put out the feed for the reindeer, and cookies and eggnog for Santa Claus."

Mrs Barnett smiled fondly at her husband. "I think you're right, suga. Come on, Nate. You're not fixin' to sit in that chair all night sulking, are you?" Mr Barnett helped the grumbling man to his feet. With quick kisses and promises to be back first thing to help celebrate Christmas, they were gone.

"If I hadn't made it in time, if he'd hurt you, I—" Markus's throat closed, the agony of what might have been unbearable.

"I was so scared, and then you came and I knew I was going to be okay, that you wouldn't let anything happen to me." The words spilled out, tumbling and falling into the silence between them. "And then I was so scared for you." Tears glistened, muddying her eyes.

"Don't you know that only the good die young? And I remember a certain country singer delighting in telling me how much of a jerk I am on more than one occasion." A thought sent his mouth twitching uncontrollably until he threw his head back and roared with laughter, albeit with more than a little hysteria.

Presley stared at him like he'd lost his mind and began to inch toward the emergency call button, obviously thinking he was having a reaction to the drugs in his system. Her huge baffled eyes only drove the hysteria further until he was gulping in air between bursts of laughter. Giving a final chortle, he wiped at his eyes. "I'm sorry, but it suddenly occurred to me that, after Paul, maybe Kelly wasn't such a bad employee after all."

"Of course she wasn't. And I can't wait to catch up with her after all this."

Alarm spiked through him, making all traces of merriment vanish. "Say what?"

"In the new year, I have a couple of days off and I've arranged to go visit her."

"I'm not going. One of the happiest days of my life was never having to see her again."

Presley shrugged. "I didn't ask you to."

"I mean, I don't even like Colorado."

"I'm sure I'll manage to get there by myself."

"I could let you use my plane."

"That would be nice."

"But I don't really like people using my plane without me."

Presley's expression grew outraged and she gave his good arm a gentle tap. "Hey, I'm not people, and you let Nate fly here on it without you."

"Nate's a very tidy man, and you're my people."

Presley's eyes softened. "Did you just call me your people?"

"If that's all right with you?"

She gave a little sniffle. "It's more than all right." She settled back into her chair. "You know, this has to be the weirdest Christmas I've ever had."

"I was just thinking that earlier."

Presley gave Markus a smile that sent his pulse racing. "I think it might be my favorite so far."

"Really?"

"Really."

"I don't have much experience with Christmases and all that, but I think I agree with you. It's the first one that ever meant anything to me." With a grunt of pain, he rolled onto his side to better look at her. "I'm still going to be me. I'm still going to be that jerk. But this jerk loves you."

Presley gave him a watery smile, her eyes shimmering. "I don't know if you realized, but I'm one of the few people who never really cared that you are you. I love you, too."

She released his hand and stood, quickly walking away from him. Markus, having never sworn his love for anyone, was left momentarily confused. Surely the woman wasn't meant to run away after a declaration, right? Presley returned with something hidden in her hands. Giving him an impish grin, she held it high above his head.

"Is that what I think it is?" Markus's reaction seemed to amuse her.

"If you think it's mistletoe, then you'd be right."

Laughter floated up from his throat. "Does anyone actually do that?"

The look she gave him was pure feminine challenge. "Oh, you'd be surprised. Now, are you going to let me share some Christmas spirit with you or not?"

For the first time ever in his life, Markus decided not to argue with the hand he'd been dealt.

THE END

As an Indie Author, reviews help me get my books noticed. If you enjoyed reading Markus and Presley's story as much as I did writing it, please leave a review. It will make all the difference to me.

If you loved, *Mistletoe and the Billionaire's Cowgirl,* sign up for my newsletter to get updates on new releases as well as exclusive extras.

Now, turn the page to discover the Billionaire Hearts Ranch, beginning with Colt.

SNEAK PEEK – THE WOUNDED COWBOY BILLIONAIRE

The sky was clean and bright, barely a cloud in the sky as Colt swung the rope experimentally, warming up as he walked his horse around. The cute cowgirl coming from the other way recognized him, her eyes widening gratifyingly and her gaze dropping to take in his gleaming gold world champion buckle. He sent her his best slow and lazy smile, cocking his head as he appraised her appreciatively, promising himself that he would catch up with her later and get to know her better.

It was a good day to be alive. Big Wheels, his horse, was calm and steady beneath him, too much of an old rodeo hand to be bothered with nerves. A movement at the edge of the warmup area caught his attention. Standing to her full five foot three inches high, his sister waved, pausing to see if he'd noticed her before setting off waving again. Beside Indie, standing tall, was his best friend—her fiancé—Bennett. Grinning at them, he loped Big Wheels over.

"I didn't expect to see you guys here. I hope someone is looking after my ranch."

Indie cocked her head at him. "The ranch is fine. Maybe

we just wanted to come and spend some time with you. You know, live the playboy billionaire lifestyle." She looked up at Bennett, a silly smile on her face. "Can we just tell him already?"

Bennett's smile was just as goofy. "If you don't, I will."

"Is someone going to tell me? Why didn't you just call me and tell me if you had something to say?" His sister looked like she was about to explode with whatever news she had to tell. Maybe he should torment her a little longer, string it out. Really, what kind of big brother wouldn't take advantage of this situation?

"We didn't want to tell you over the phone. This is something that I wanted to see your face when we told you. You're the only family I have, and I want to do this right."

"You guys didn't run off and get married, did you? Bennett, you and I are going to have words if you didn't give my little sister the big wedding she's always dreamed of."

Bennet exchanged a knowing look with him. "You think she'd let me get away with an elopement?"

Colt chuckled. "Maybe not. So, what's this big news you're all fired up to tell me about?"

Indie's eyes shimmered with excitement, and she clutched at Bennett's arm as if to anchor herself and not get carried away with her emotions. "Colt, I'm pregnant. We're going to be having a baby." Colt felt like he'd been poleaxed. His baby sister was going to have a baby. A bittersweet wave hit him. *Mom would have loved being a grandma.* "You are happy for us, aren't you, Colt?" Indie's eyes no longer shimmered with excitement, but now tears threatened.

"You caught me by surprise, but I like the idea of being Uncle Colt." He slid off his horse and wrapped her up in a giant bear hug. "You're going to make the best mom," he whispered in her ear.

He shook Bennett's hand. "Congratulations. I'm over the moon for you guys."

Bennett's grip was firm. "Thanks. You know I'll make sure they never want for anything."

"If I'd had my doubts, I wouldn't have let you anywhere near her when we were in high school." Colt's name crackled over the loudspeaker. "I'm next in. Are you guys staying around?"

"Yeah, this one here"—Bennett smiled lovingly down at Indie—"informs me that she already has cravings. So, we'll stay for the rodeo and then head home afterwards."

Indie punched her fiancé lightly on the arm. "Hey, mister, these cravings are real. Now, enough with this chitchat. Colt, go catch a steer, and you"—she crooked her finger at Bennett—"need to go hunt me down some pickles, corndogs and ice cream."

"That seems fair enough," Colt said, climbing back into the saddle.

"She plans on eating them all together like one big pickle-corndog sundae." Bennett shuddered at the thought.

Colt grimaced, staring in horror at his sister. "Indie, that's gross."

"And I don't care. Now, git." She shooed him away with her hands.

Colt could feel a gooey smile on his face. Well, how about that? His baby sister was having a baby, and with one of his best friends, no less.

Check out Colt's story, *The Wounded Cowboy Billionaire Cowboy* available on Amazon

ACKNOWLEDGMENTS

A debt of gratitude to my editor Rebekah Groves for her patience with me.

Another big thanks to Megan from Designed with Grace for her cover design.

To my amazing beta readers and street team, you guys rock and I couldn't do it without you. Special mention to Lisa and Cair.

And finally to my fabulous alpha reader Trixie Norman, for all the late nights of reading and endless questions about your thoughts.

A cowgirl's passion

One feisty cowgirl. One steadfast Brazilian bull rider. Will she see what is right in front of her?

Buy Now

A cowgirl's pride

An Aussie cowgirl from the wrong side of the tracks. A handsome equine vet. Can they find a way to have their happy ever after?

Buy Now

A cowgirl's love

A young Aussie cowgirl. A widowed rancher. Does age matter when it comes to love?

Buy Now

A cowgirl's movie star

A fiery cowgirl with big dreams. A movie star far from home. When their two worlds collide, will their love be strong enough to hold them together or will they be pulled apart

Buy Now

A cowgirl's billionaire

A cowgirl adrift. A broken billionaire cowboy. Can he free himself from the past to be the man she needs now?

Buy Now

Cowboy Christmas Series

The Mistletoe Collection

Boots and Mistletoe

Cowboy boots, mistletoe, and a holiday do-over…

Buy Now

The Cowboy Under the Mistletoe

It'll take more than the magic of the season to help this grump find her happily ever after…

Buy Now

Mistletoe and the Billionaire's Cowgirl

He's the last man she wants this holiday season. Too bad he's exactly what she needs…

Buy Now

ABOUT THE AUTHOR

Edith MacKenzie or Eddie Mac to her friends is an author of sweet and wholesome contemporary cowboy romance. They say in literary circles to write what you know, and Eddie has certainly taken that to heart. Before embarking on a writing career, she trained horses professionally and brings that wealth of knowledge to her writing.

Now a mum to a boy and girl, as well as wife, she delights with her tales of strong cowgirls and their adventures in finding love. When not weaving the love stories of her characters, she enjoys hanging out with her family and animals, as well as reading, fishing and camping.

Just remember—once a cowgirl, always a cowgirl.

facebook.com/EddieMacAuthor

instagram.com/edith_mackenzie_author

amazon.com/Edith-MacKenzie

bookbub.com/profile/edith-mackenzie

twitter.com/edith_mackenzie